One Night in Warsaw

Erica Vipond

Cover Art: Lauren Bencivengo (@Carmela_designs)

Cover Designer: Erica Vipond

Copyeditor: Miranda Mullings (@Mirandadoescopy)

ISBN 979-8-218-82899-8

ASIN B0FX538VQL (ebook)

Also by Erica Vipond

Starling Darling

WHAT PEOPLE ARE SAYING

ABOUT STARLING DARLING

"Beautiful, a stunning tribute to the fractured relationships between mothers and daughters. Absolutely, phenomenal women's fiction. Literature I will highly recommend for years to come."

— Sunny

"I have never been to Rome before...but I think I would like to go to the Rome that Erica Vipond describes. In fact, I think her greatest strength lies in describing locations and conjuring atmospheres."

— Shannon

"The writing is so eloquent and poetic. A wonderful depiction of grief and love. A story about forgiveness, self-love, and empathy. LOVED. can't wait for more books by Erica."

— Sydney

Contents

Content Note

Amara's cottage is set in France, largely inspired by Aix-en-Provence, as well as the respective beauty of Warsaw and London. All flattering details in the story were inspiration drawn from each place, while any flaws portrayed are simply a result of my own active imagination.

This book contains elements that may not be suitable for all readers, including sexual content, strong language, and brief, non-specific references of murder of children, but does not depict the aforementioned subject graphically. This book contains references to abandonment, grief, and death. Please read with care.

To Dar;

For your fierceness

and to Kristin;

For your friendship.

The geography never matters.

Chapter One

South of France, Present day

I draw closer to a dilapidated cottage, my deliberate steps a whisper on the ground. Squinting into the dark surroundings, there is only the swaying of trees and insects chittering in the late hour of the French countryside, although fear, cold as ice, clings to my spine like frost on spindly branches. Just beyond an iron gate is a front garden bathed in silvery rays of moonlight. Paint on the front door is peeling along its edges like a shipwreck left for decades in a field. My fingernails dig into my palms at my sides as I try to calm my trembling. I move through dense, prickly stems of tall grass, stalks left to grow wild and untamed. Scanning the field for movement, paranoia beats in me like a drum.

Hesitantly, I push open the vine-tangled gate. A loud groan of rusted hinges is a knife slicing through the night. My hands halt, gripping the cool iron. My eyes dart in every direction. Despite the chilly air of late autumn, dark tendrils of hair cling to my neck in a cold sweat. Every muscle is on alert. *Breathe*, I tell myself, as if I can will myself to stop shaking. The night contains my terror: shadows, uncertainty of what might happen to me. What if I'm not alone?

When the only sounds I hear are the white noise of the countryside, I forge ahead. After a 13-hour trek from London, fatigue and desperation pull me toward the dark cottage with hope for a safe place to sleep. Now past the gate, a winding cobble path leads me to the front door. My eyes begin to adjust to the shadows, details emerging slowly like film developing in a dark room. Untended what stalks rustle beneath windows on the far left side, closer to the road. Empty terra-cotta pots lie on their sides, earth taking over clay. I slowly turn the bronzed knob of the front door, but it refuses to budge. Goddammit. Grunting against it, my efforts are as futile as pushing against a cement wall. Unmoveable. I try to think through my panic.

Where's the key where's the key where's the key?

I'd inadvertently left the map with its written instructions in the car, and attempt to recall them now. Warily, I look in the direction of the parked car on the gravel drive, just beyond the noisy gate. Fumbling in the dark will only draw more attention.

I remember a scribbled note on the map—a key hidden in a pot on the east side of the house, directly below a window. Weeds snap beneath my feet as my fingers trail along rough stone. Peering into the first two windows, I squint through opaque glass, aging dirt and dust obscuring any view inside. At a third window, I find a pot sitting atop a garden stone. It is a perfectly preserved sunflower. In the dark, metal shines through the small peephole at the bottom of the pot. Tossing out its contents, I rummage blindly, fingers scattering among the wreckage of dirt to grasp the key. I follow the path

I'd made in reverse toward the front door. Key in hand, a muffling click sounds, though the door still doesn't budge. It could be stuck in its frame from disuse or perhaps secured by a secondary interior lock. Adrenaline evaporates into helplessness. Had I driven all this way simply to fail? Leaning my forehead against the peeling door, I pound my fists against it. Stifling a scream in my throat, I sound like a wounded animal. Underneath my jacket is a bloodstain from London that will never wash out. Nausea threatens to pull me under its murky surface. I don't want to think about the consequences of decisions that led me here, though I feel ill-equipped to face them now. I'm just a desk jockey. A career solicitor in MI6 with expertise specific only to legal challenges or complex legislative changes. I'm not trained for something like this. I am one failure away from collapsing in the shadows of this forgotten, decaying place.

In my pocket, no larger than my palm, is a device so precious that it would be the end of me if anything happened to it. Pressure mounts in my chest as regret for what happened in London threatens my vision. The burden of it in my pocket is both a terrifying and reassuring weight. I can't forget why I'm here and what's at stake. I can't forget what it cost. Shuddering out a breath, I work to gather myself as turmoil spins me in its grip. *Focus.* I grit my teeth against the strain of it. *Think of what you need to do next.*

Wrestling my full weight against the door, I dig a shoulder into the wood. With a final burst of strength, it finally gives way. A shooting pain, brief and sharp, travels down my arm as an empty front room greets me. I squeeze a hand against my shoulder. Quickly retrieving my most lethal—and only—weapon, my hand grips the handle of a slim knife. A dull blade only sharp enough to appear threatening and barely serrated enough to saw through food. It's useless, but it's all I have.

Hesitantly, I shuffle a few steps inside. A musky smell permeates the cottage, a smell of mold and abandonment. Fear spikes into my spine like a stake. Placing one tentative foot in front of the other, I scrape along the woodgrain of the floor. A nearby light switch fails to work. My hands swat through cobwebs, their delicate and sticky threads sticking to my sweaty skin. With a cough and a wave, I make my way deeper into the house.

Through a gleam of moonlight, a lone candlestick lies on its side. Retrieving a matchbook from my other pocket, I rattle the cardboard even though I already know there are only a few remaining matchsticks. I ignite one against the striker strip, orange flame reflecting in the window. Its shape is a blur in the glass's grimy film. I carry the candlestick down the length of the narrow hallway, my heart pounding. A tightness between my shoulder blades tells me to stay vigilant.

As I reach the furthest room in the back, a crashing sound echoes from the front of the cottage. All sense of logic evaporates completely. Gripping the knife in my hand, my body goes entirely cold.

It could be anything.

Anyone.

It could be a member of Tatrialny, playing games in the shadows as they wait for me to find them in the dark.

It's difficult to see anything clearly. Do I escape through a back window? What do I do? I want someone to tell me. I want someone else to make these decisions that might be life or death.

Just then, movement glints in the shadows as something comes toward me in the hall. I choke on a scream.

A chicken appears at my feet. I seem to startle it as much as it does me. It releases an upsetting, squawking shriek, its feathery wings fluttering at the shock of someone else being in the house.

My hand flies up to my mouth from the near collision. On spindly legs, the bird scratches at the surface of a table in the corner of the front room, and my fear spirals into mania as I devolve into a fit of hysterical laughter. I clutch my hands against my mouth as I sink to the ground. The pitching sound of my own laughter, unnaturally high, gives way to trembling sobs. The bird bobs its head curiously at me.

Despite escaping London through the Channel Tunnel unseen, driving across France, and protecting tech that could surely get me killed, a bird found its way inside this place more easily than I had. How the hell am I going to survive what comes next?

Wiping my cheeks with the back of my hand, I push myself onto steadier feet. I have to keep going. As dawn breaks on the distant horizon, I blow out the candle and pace back to the car to retrieve my belongings. Gingerly setting my two duffel bags inside the cottage, a small plume of dust rises, static and stale in the air. Rummaging in the half-light of the kitchen, I sort through the contents of the larger one. Enough euros to last me a few years, toiletries, and three passports with three false identities. I shiver in the icy air as I trade my sweater for something clean. A chasm grows inside my chest at the reminder of the bloodstain on its sleeve. Like so much else, I need to rid myself of it.

Locating a half-empty can of petrol in the cupboard, I bring a metal bin around outside. Other than a few scattered houses in the distance, I have complete privacy.

Tossing my clothes into the bin, I coat them with liquid. The smell of it stings my nose. I hold the small matchbox in my palm and strike its last match. I read its tender inscription, handwritten on plain cardboard—both a confession and a promise:

Tu étais où pendant tout ce temps?

Where have you been all my life?

Having come into this world an orphan, I know what it is to truly feel alone. So why is this part the most difficult? The low flame is a taunting funeral procession licking at the air. For one heart-wrenching breath, I stand on the precipice of what is necessary to do. At its terrifying edge, I must jump off the cliff. Otherwise, this will all have been for nothing.

I toss the box in, watching every last shred of me that is good burn along with it. Everything could have been different if Emerson had made different choices. The sweater with its bloodstains and memories furls black until it finally relinquishes to the flame. The heat of it briefly warms my skin from the air of an impending winter, as visible now as the sun is on the horizon. Placing the cover for the bin before the plumes of smoke give me away, I know this is only the beginning. There's the matter of the device, the state of the cottage, and most importantly, ensuring no one finds me here. I've never been well-versed in disaster, and Emerson, the one person who could have helped me, is dead.

Chapter Two

Warsaw, Poland, Six months earlier

Nearing the iron gate in the front of a children's home, the ambient noise of the city hums at my back. My eyes lift upwards at the stone building before me, and I contemplate its wide doors separating what's inside from the rest of the world. Nearby birds fly up to the morning sky, fluttering their wings. Each hinge of the gate creaks softly as I close it behind me. Warsaw has been a twenty-five-year odyssey. This is my only chance to find out who my birth parents are. Torn between what I want to know and what I'm afraid to find out, I hesitate with anticipation that sits like a rock in the pit of my stomach. Not knowing won't make the truth less real. The only difference is that once I know, I can never go back to unknowing.

The heels of my shoes scuff against stone as I ascend a small set of stairs to the door. There isn't much to the edifice of the building. Its form is common to the capital, with scaffolding and architecture rebuilt for function after the destruction during the Second World War. On the landing, there's nothing more than leafy plants with foliage the shape of hearts, and a gold doorbell, faded from touch and time. Suddenly, a chime sounds from my bag. I recognize the text notification and ignore it. If it's my friend James, I'll answer later. When I begin to reach for the doorbell, my phone chimes a second time. It's a text from Henry Clark, and my heart slams into my chest at the sight of his name. The shock of it has my finger hovering over the screen to read what he has to say, but I stop myself. Hardening with outrage, I can't believe he has the audacity to contact me after all this time. It had taken months to forget about those few weeks we'd spent together. About how good it'd felt with him. The nights his mouth had lingered between my trembling legs. How funny he was. I had felt alive and safe and free. Until I'd seen him with another woman one night. Her hands around his neck and her lips against his mouth with such obvious familiarity, I wanted to fling them both off Tower Bridge. An unlucky coincidence of time and place that led me to witness him. That night, I sent him a message that it was over, then refused every one of his calls. I didn't want to hear attempts at defense or explanation. To block him out and forget him was a switch easily levered after a lifetime of practice. His betrayal only confirmed what I had seen in life: no one will protect you better than you can protect yourself, so you must be the one to do it.

I shove my phone back inside my purse and flip the ring switch off without another glance. I set my bag down and sit on the stoop, facing the street. I drag a hand through my hair and let out a sigh. A yellow tram glides past, full of morning commuters. The neighborhood is a juxtaposition of graffiti and hardy bushes able to survive winter.

My phone vibrates again, though it's more prolonged, indicating a call. I'm fighting irritation until I see the name on the screen is Emerson Charles, Chief of the Secret Intelligence Office. A man appointed by *the* Foreign Secretary. My boss's boss at MI6, and technically, my former mentor. I answer the call without delay.

"Emerson," I say in greeting, curiosity masking concern. "I'm surprised to hear from you. Is everything all right with Helen?"

"She's good, though I know she'll give me a hard time if I don't come back with something to tell her about you when she asks," Emerson says about his wife, though he sounds slightly distracted. A door closes in the background. "I trust you're enjoying Warsaw?"

"It's nice here in the spring," I say, propping my chin on my hand. I had been reticent to share the purpose of my trip to anyone except James, but I suspect Emerson knows, given that he knows I was adopted in Warsaw. "Might take a walk through the Old Town later, maybe see a museum." I pause. "But I don't think you're curious about my tourist stops."

He lets out an assenting sigh. "Spot on, so I'll get right to it," he says. "There's an investigation requiring some legal cross-checking. You're the most suited to parse through the details. There's also a sensitive nature to it, and a degree of urgency. We—*I*, could use your insight as to potential implications of this case."

My mind instinctively dashes to every possibility. Aside from James, Emerson is the only other person whose integrity I can trust, though I keep in mind the decisions he makes when navigating security operations. Despite his cordial tone, it must be something truly urgent for him to be calling me right now. In my five years as a solicitor at MI6, work has rarely interrupted my personal life. In fact, my personal life has always been steadfastly separate from work.

Well, except for that one time.

"What do you need from me, sir?" I ask.

"It's delicately complex, and not something we can get into at the moment. You mentioned the Old Town—can you be at Market Square in two hours?"

"Two hours," I repeat, glancing at my screen to check the time. "No problem, I'll be there."

"Excellent. I'll contact you then," says Emerson. The line disconnects before I can ask why he needs to call me from the Old Town.

I shake my head to clear it. Returning my phone to the inside pocket of my bag, I rise from my seat on the steps and turn to face the door. I had lived here and I had left it, far too young to know what questions to ask. If there was ever a moment to decide, now was it.

My fingers press the doorbell. The deep and echoing chime from behind the closed doors reminds me of a church. There's a faint clack of heels, then a woman. She studies me politely. She's smaller than I am, her silver hair in a tidy chignon that reminds me of a nun, even though I know I know this is a secular orphanage. I do a fast calculation. She might be the right age to have been here when I was younger. Should her face be one I can recognize?

"*Czy mogę ci pomóc?*" she says, asking if she can help me.

"I'm hoping to speak with someone about being adopted from

here," I reply in Polish. I offer a warm smile, though I fear it's more tense than I intend. She peers around the sides of me, as if expecting someone else to be there.

"We didn't have anyone scheduled today. Did you make an appointment?"

"I didn't," I reply with confusion.

"You can make an appointment online, and come back then," she tells me politely, hands on the door. "Thank you, have a nice day."

It takes me an overlong moment to realize she's shutting the door until it's nearly closed.

"Wait!" I press against the door with both my palms and an uneven kind of desperation. "I'm not here to adopt. *I* was adopted from here."

The woman pulls the door further ajar as she stares at me in puzzlement. I wonder what she sees. Are there remaining traces of my loneliness, or has it all melted away over time while I rebuilt myself across the Atlantic? She must find whatever she's looking for in my expression, because she swings the door inward and gestures for me to enter.

"Please, come in," she says. "Many leave, though they don't usually return. I will help however I can."

"Thank you," I say and take a few steps into the entryway.

Sliding the lock, she begins walking down a bright and narrow hallway. "The office is there."

She doesn't check behind her to see if I'm following, though of course I am. Before I'd left London, I had imagined everything except for this: I might ask questions of the staff, but how would I feel about the answers? I am made of glass as I follow after her.

We arrive in the cool air of an office with a singular window. The shutters are open to the street. She points to the chair across the desk. Striped roman shades are pulled up high, their elegance incongruous to the metal file cabinets, which stand flush against the back wall. The woman folds open a laptop on the desk before turning her attention back to me.

"Tell me more, my dear. You would like to know something about your adoption?" Her voice fills with patience, though a lack of curiosity. For me, this was a home, but for her, this is only a job.

"I'm hoping you can tell me any information about my birth parents," I reply.

"Do you know who adopted you from here?" Her hands fold across the desk. "Their names?"

"Yes," I say with a nod. "Rhodes, with an *h*. Harper and William Rhodes."

She spends a few minutes tapping on the keyboard of her laptop. It feels impersonal to make introductions of each other's names now, and I wish I'd asked at the start. Her hands turn the screen of the laptop to face me. A red error message hangs above a search bar, the page empty.

"There's nothing I can find," she says. "When were you adopted?"

"It would have been 25 years ago," I tell her.

"Not all records have been digitized," she breaks to me gently.

"This would not go back that far." She points to the laptop with a kind of finality that dashes any hope that has survived my journey here.

"I was raised by the couple who adopted me," I say in a clear voice, intent on staying strong. "I lived with my parents until they passed away a few years ago. I have no one else. If I have any biological family who are alive, I want to know I'm not the only one." I swallow my pride. "Please help me."

"You only lived with them—the Rhodes? No other family?" she asks. "You speak Polish very well."

"Only them," I confirm with a nod. "My parents greatly admired the people of Poland and felt it was important to stay connected to my country by maintaining the language. They didn't want me to feel as if I'd been pulled from everything. My mother made sure I had a tutor to teach me."

"They sound wonderful. Not all are so lucky," she says with a hint of sadness.

"I was very lucky," I say thickly.

"I cannot guarantee we have what you are looking for, but let me check." She shuffles to the file cabinets. "Do you know if you were given a different name back then?"

"Yes," I say, there's a spark of memory, like a wildfire burning across a field, rushing to meet me. "My name used to be Ada. My parents wanted to keep my new name somewhat similar."

Turning to the fourth set of file cabinets, she mutters to herself while thumbing through assorted folder tabs. I can't see much from where I sit. My fingers twist around my sweater's sleeve as I wait. After several moments, she huffs a noise of triumph before turning back to sit. She places a single folder on her desk and retrieves a pair of wire-rimmed glasses from a drawer.

She reads aloud in a barely audible volume, and I lean in to try to hear. "*...Ada... outside...*" Her unpainted fingernails scan across the page, flipping back and forth. The folder itself is thin, no more than ten pages long. Nothing more to show for the first six years of my life than yellowing paper stuck in a metal file cabinet. Lifting her head, she meets my gaze.

"You were found, perhaps only hours old, at the front door."

"Found?"

She waves in the direction of the front door as she continues reading notes. "A woman brought you here. Someone young, I think maybe your mother. It was assumed so, since you were only a newborn."

I don't know why it takes me by surprise. Even though I was only a few hours old, my own mother hadn't wanted me. Of course she gave me up. How else could I have gotten here?

"Is there anything else you can tell me?" I ask.

She leans back in her leather chair. "These are very old notes. The requirements were different back then for children who were surrendered."

A flicker of disappointment must cross my face because she reaches for a pen and paper, pushing it toward me.

"A woman who worked here before, Irena, might have information. I can speak with her and ask if she remembers something else that might help."

There's an unceremonious quality to her delivery, but her eyes are kind. I write my name and number on the sheet of paper and hand it back to her. After shaking her hand, I retreat out into the street. The door closes behind me with a sinking sense of finality. My feet are once again on the steps from where I had ascended only a half hour earlier. Making my way in the direction of the Old Town Market Square, I'm relieved my eyes are completely dry. There's not even a threat of a tear.

Maybe I'll never find out who brought me into this world—only that I was left in it without them. Numbness deprives me of having a strong reaction. It can't be a shock if this is what I had anticipated, right? It isn't sadness, either. I have lived with this concave awareness my entire life. Over the years, there's been an ebb and flow to it, like water sloshing clumsily in a sphere, vertical enough for me to wade in, deep enough to drown. Sadness would be easier, I think. It would at least be something I can name.

When I arrive in the square, the area is milling with pedestrians and cyclists. Buildings loom like giants over souvenir shops and families walking about. With a glance at my watch, I notice there's still a little more time before I can expect Emerson's call.

I take a seat beneath the shade of a terrace and order a beverage. Crowds trickle over the sidewalks. I take a deep drink from my glass. I had long imagined what it would be like to be in Warsaw, but reality is far stranger, far harsher, here in daylight.

Emerson's call comes in right on the dot of two hours. He returns to the conversation as if we'd never left it.

"One of our field agents is going to debrief you."

That part surprises me, but I adapt quickly. "Do we know when they'll be making contact?"

"Shortly." With a sigh, he adds, "I'm sorry to cut your holiday short. I know this trip was important." I've always admired Emerson's ability to tap into sincerity despite the stress of his position in MI6. I know that his authority generates a powerful reputation for the UK's strongest agency, and it makes me even more curious about the nature of this case he's asking me to help with.

"It's quite all right," I say, meaning it. I will take any distraction from the deluge of thoughts after this morning. "Which agent will be contacting me?"

"Agent Clark," he replies. "I believe you're familiar with him from a separate case."

I choke back a cough and set my drink down. "Yes. We met last fall," I say. It takes everything in me to keep my voice casually passive.

"He'll give you a brief overview, and you'll get a chance to read the documents. He'll share access from an encrypted file." I hear a rustling of a keyboard. "Clark has full domestic and international clearance, so any advisement you give him he'll later run up to me when he returns to headquarters."

"For a video meeting?" I ask, a crease of confusion forming between my brows.

"It will be in-person," clarifies Emerson.

My jaw falls open as I look around, but there are only people in groups and pairs walking along the sidewalk. Despite our friendship, he is the one leading MI6, and so I'm reluctant to draw too much attention to my resistance to meet with Henry. Or worse, be forced to reveal why if Emerson asked. I make one last appeal to his pragmatism.

"It's no problem for me to return for debrief in London," I say, my stomach dropping lower. "The flight's only a few hours."

"Due to his geographical proximity, contacting you directly was the most logical step," says Emerson. His tone is straightforward, but it carries the authority to quiet any further pushback. I'm still processing this appalling announcement when Emerson begins to wrap up our call.

"I'm stepping into a meeting. For now, keep your response and evaluations off email and messaging."

There's quiet static where instructions had been, just a beat before a voice, deep and sonorous, speaks behind me.

"Hello, Amara, darling."

I startle at the distinct London lilt. I hadn't noticed anyone approaching. Half-turning in my chair, my eyes meet the man standing before me. With hands in his front pockets and a head full of dark hair curving over his brow, he holds my astonished look with his eyes.

"I believe you were looking for me."

I should have known, even then, that the devil could be out in daylight.

Chapter Three

South of France, Present Day

The sun emerges like a blade cutting into dusty shadows in the cold of this forsaken cottage. Flares of light bathe the front room where I'd been sleeping. Squinting, I feel as if I've been hit by a car. When I sit up on the thin pallet I'd slept on, the coat I'd used as a blanket slides off onto the floor. The beginning of a headache presses at the back of my skull.

I yelp when I realize the chicken is in the room. It watches me with an unblinking stare. Its speckled brown feathers blend into the wood stain of the table. Each wing curls against its side.

Surveying the space in daylight is a far different experience than at night. The space is in a far worse state of disrepair than I'd initially thought. A side table stands with a crack in its front leg. Paint peeling off a patina wall suggests it had been coral once. Magazine pages are strewn along the floor. An old, upright piano sits in a corner, a layer of dust covering the frame. It's missing a key like a gaping tooth. Putting my coat on for warmth, I sort through the rest of the house. I notice for the first time a greenhouse sitting at the bottom of a slope down from the cottage. It's far enough from the road to be mostly out of sight. It appears empty, clearly worn away by however many seasons it's been there. Something to investigate later.

In the one bathroom, the barest essentials include a working porcelain sink, tub, and toilet. Both bedrooms are empty, and I make my way to the kitchen near the front room. With my hunger a hollow tomb in my belly, I open every cupboard and every drawer in search of something to eat. A short while later, I survey my pile on the kitchen island: a can of chickpeas, a bottle of dish soap, two cans of lentils, matzo crackers, and the remaining dregs of red wine. My stomach sinks with desperation. I sniff the packet of crackers. Choosing ignorance, I decide not to check the expiration date and take a bite. My restless fingers tap against the counter while I study my crinkled map. To the west is a small lake, while to the east is a nearby town. When I smell something funny, I'm horrified to realize it's me. Eyeing the bathroom, I sniff my sweater again and decide it's probably worth the risk. I don't want to attract *more* attention when I go to town for food.

I breathe through my mouth at the smell of mildew. Crouching down toward the faucet, I grip the knob. I huff through the effort of turning past rust until it finally relents. Pipes groan as the water pours out, brown at first, then after a few minutes, turning clear. My fingers recoil from the frigid temperature of the water. All I have is dish soap, and I long for the soft scents of soap at my flat. Straightening, I wonder if the love of my adopted family had made me soft. Had life not made me hardened enough to tolerate my grim situation? I decide then and there to stop mourning my life in London if I want to get through this. Sentimentality will get me killed.

Briskly removing my clothes, I step into the stream of the showerhead. The cold water is a shock, and my body involuntarily locks up. I tilt the shower head as close to the middle of the clawfoot tub as I can to avoid splashing water everywhere. The past washes down the drain in a diluted line beneath my feet. I begin to shiver violently and quickly emulsify soap in my hands.

Once I'm clothed, I grab the car keys and the duffel containing the device, passports, and money. As I'm nearly out the door, I realize the bird is still watching me. I try to shoo it outside, its fluttering squawks warning me loudly, an aggressive remark that says, *it's more comfortable here than out there.*

"You'll have to leave eventually," I say scornfully.

Reversing the car down the long, pebble driveway, I pull out into the road toward town. Blue sky stretches over the landscape as I drive past crumbling Roman walls and hilltop villages. The car tires kick up autumn leaves, scattering the ground beneath it. Olive groves dance in the wind. Cypress trees stand in the distance like arrows aiming toward the sun. Time has left its mark on the rest of the world, but not in this corner of earth, where wildness springs up around untamed lavender fields. The idyllic landscape of the Luberon is, in another life, a dreamy place to be. For me, it is damnation.

As I near the town, roads begin to narrow and become more precise. Parking as close as I can to the main part of the village, there is a smattering of patrons sipping coffee on terraces, and vendors exchanging goods for money. Sunlight glints off terra-cotta shingles and muted, pale-white shutters. Yet, even the lively fluctuations of noise coursing through the streets aren't enough to distract me from my hunger and thirst. Catching sight of a fruit and vegetable display, assortments of bins follow along a stretch of sidewalk. Past a vet office is a sizable supermarket. Hungry for everything, I fill every corner of a cart with fruits, vegetables, bottles of water, cleaning supplies, and dry goods. Thinking of the stupid chicken, I throw in a bundle of leafy greens. It's only because I don't want the nuisance of a hungry animal pestering me for my own food. As the cashier begins scanning items, I wonder how much of me they might remember, or if I'll simply be assumed for any of the faceless and nameless tourists who come through. Getting to France was as far as any semblance of plans went. The rest—keeping the device protected and finding a way to access the data—was my only priority. In addition to not getting killed.

I load the car quickly. Inside, I shove a handful of blueberries into my mouth as I navigate back to the cottage. With one hand on the wheel, I reach for another handful. By the time I pull into the drive of the cottage, the berries are gone. I put the car in park and let out a sigh. A wall of stone laced with wisteria surrounds the front yard. The greenhouse sits quietly just beyond it. My eyes scan the area until I catch sight of myself in the rearview mirror. I had slept poorly the night before. Dark smudges crease under my hazel eyes, giving me away. Tendrils of tousled hair have fallen out of my braid. I trace a finger along a jagged, raised scar that runs along my hairline, just over my left ear. Pushing the mirror back and out of sight, I turn away, not wanting the reminder or the memories.

CHAPTER FOUR

WARSAW, POLAND, SIX MONTHS EARLIER

"Henry," I say stiffly. Shielding my eyes, I peer up at him as the afternoon sun haloes his head.

"Always lovely to see you," he says with an appraising look. Perhaps a random bystander might find the tenor of his voice warm, enticing. But I know better.

He pulls out the chair across from mine and leans back, stretching his long legs with an easy smile. The blue of his shirt stretches across his broad shoulders. My eyes slide over to him coldly. Not even bothering to conceal a scowl, I tug at the cardigan I'd draped over the chair he's currently sitting in.

"I see you make yourself comfortable everywhere, not only at headquarters."

"You've gotten a bit of rest since I last saw you," he says. He gestures to a waiter for attention.

"I can't recall when that was," I say with an arching brow, "as it tends not to register on any scale of importance."

The flash of white when he smiles makes him look even more smug and arrogant. His dark hair sweeps across his forehead with a light breeze. When a waiter approaches asking what we'd like to order, Henry wastes no time.

"Yes, one Tyskie, *proszę*. For you, Amara?"

Conflicted, I want to avoid sitting here any longer than obligated. But if I must, then a drink will be absolutely necessary. With a polite smile, I motion to my empty glass.

"Another Babuni, please," I say to the waiter. "Strawberry."

As they walk away with our drink orders, another smile begins to curl on Henry's lips.

"What?" I ask with annoyance.

"Very classy and sweet."

"I understand you'll flirt with a house plant, but do try and keep this professional," I say, waving a finger between us.

"I was only referring to the wine," he says, raising his palms innocently.

"Mmhm." I turn my attention out to the square. His presence is both distracting and unsettling. It makes this trip, which was already difficult, even less pleasant.

"Can I at least apologize?" His offer breaks the silence.

"No," I tell him, looking over my glass as I nonchalantly take a sip. "I quite like to hold a grudge."

"If we cleared the air," he says, "we could finally come to an understanding about what happened, and—"

I recoil at the suggestion. "That is *not* what we're here to discuss."

Were it not for the intensity of his watchful gaze, he would appear to be the convincing image of relaxation, his hand on his drink, his white button-down fluttering in the spring air.

"You didn't leave me any choice," he says lightly, his voice thinly etching out his frustration. "You rejected all my calls, my messages. I tried everything I could think of."

"Oh, yes," I say evenly, snapping forward in my seat. "You certainly *tried* convincing me you were going out of town, only for me to discover you were very much in town, with another woman." Dismay that I am litigating old resentments with him rises in my chest, growing from the size of a pebble to a boulder in a matter of moments. I let air deflate from my lungs and set aside mental images of shocking him with all the things I'd really like to say, such as, *Have you ever had to swim from being thrown off a bridge?* Or, *Did you know a person can survive an abdominal stab wound?* I wave a hand between us with an air of neutrality I do not feel. "You know what? We were never anything to begin with, so there's no reason to be upset. You were—are—free to fuck whoever you wanted."

"In town with another woman," he echoes vacantly, as if understanding is finally dawning on him for the first time. "So you did see me that night with her."

"That's what I just said," I tell him brusquely.

"I'm just trying to catch up," he tells me, the roguish tint of his tone gone. "You're wrong, though. You were entitled to know why I'd said I was going to be out of town that night. I assure you it had nothing to do with us—"

"I don't know how many ways to say it," I say with a sharp inhale, "but I'm not interested in discussing *anything* beyond the obligations of Vauxhall Cross."

Our drinks have the unfortunate timing of arriving just then, and the waiter discreetly and skittishly leaves. The break in conversation gives me a moment to get a grip on myself. This entire day has spun out of control, and it needs a bit of nudging back to normal. I only need to endure the next few hours with him, then we'll each be on our way.

"Let's finish these drinks and stick to your debrief," I suggest. "There's privacy in the lobby of the hotel I'm staying in. I can bring down my laptop to review the documents Chief mentioned."

He takes a sip of his drink, studying me across the table. "I appreciate that you take things so seriously." The laser-sharp focus of his attention annoys the hell out of me.

"Let me guess—you never do."

"It's not an insult," Henry tells me, his gaze turning toward the crowds. "Neither was the comment of looking restful. Quite the opposite, really."

His gaze turns toward the square. He was right—since last fall, we've barely had an exchange after I kept refusing his calls and refusing his gaze at the office in passing. His reputation for exacting callousness was apparent to me after that. It took a while to understand I knew more about him from others than from him directly. It was better if it stayed that way. Only after I finish my drink do I regret the warm buzz from the beverage on an empty stomach.

"I have a dinner reservation," I lie. "So perhaps we can get on with it and get through the debriefing about why you're here?"

He finishes the remaining contents in his glass. He sets a banknote of 100 *zloty* on the table.

"Shall we?"

"I'm this way," I say, indicating behind him. We walk across a footbridge that curves across the Vistula riverbank. A row of contemporary buildings comes into view of Gdańsk as we continue in silence. The city is brimming with chatter and crowds, even with dusk less than an hour away. Shadows at our feet begin to claim the golden edge of what's left of the afternoon as we continue in the direction of my hotel. There's no reason to bother asking preemptive questions about the case, as it's too crowded. We'd need more privacy to discuss any part of the case, outside of earshot on public streets. Anyway, I really don't want to converse if we don't have to.

When I recognize the angular windows of a nearby building, I point to an intersection not far from us.

"We're a few blocks from the hotel," I tell Henry. "I'm staying at the Hideaway. It's down this block and on the corner."

He falls in step beside me as we pass a gated playground. An older couple sitting on a park bench peels an orange, and I catch pieces of their conversation about their evening plans. Squeals and shrieks of children journey toward us on a breeze. Just then, two twin girls run up on the sidewalk, and one trips on an uneven jut of the concrete.

Reflexively, I reach out a hand to catch the girl by the arm. Gingerly, she accepts my hand to help her up. Wisps of golden hair cling to her cheeks, flushed from running. As she stands to her feet, I smile at her. She offers me a shy thanks, then runs to catch up to her sister.

"Is that... an actual smile?"

I whirl around. "Must you ruin everything?"

"I hadn't realized that to get through your defenses, I only needed to be a small and clumsy child," Henry teases. We're so close that I'm reminded his dark eyes are actually a deep brown, with irises that follow my movements.

"Just because you have no heart doesn't mean you mean you need to spoil things for the rest of us," I say, continuing toward the main intersection, where cars move in a roundabout. I don't bother glancing to see if he's still walking with me.

"Unfortunately, a woman who insults me to my face is a woman after my own heart," he says. A quick glance tells me he's holding his hand dramatically to his chest.

"Are you not capable of keeping it together until the hotel?" I ask with irritation.

"Did you check your pockets?" Henry changes the subject amiably.

I want to ignore him, but—*goddammit*—despite my enmity, curiosity gets the better of me.

"What are you prattling on about?" I ask in annoyance.

"A con artist the size of a child distracts you with a fall, and before you know it, the other child has already grabbed your wallet while you're looking away," Henry says. His face fills with a magnanimous sort of expression, as if he's doing me a favor with his sage observation. "Oldest play in the book."

"That is not what happened," I tell him with a scoff. "And anyway, you would've noticed because, to my unfortunate fucking luck, you are *still here*."

The quirk on his lips fades, a sober expression replacing it. "I'm only teasing, Amara."

"Well—don't." My tone comes off incisive, but at least it's honest. More than I can say for him. "I don't enjoy being toyed with."

His wolfish grin returns. "I'll try and keep the toying to a minimum."

"Jesus Christ," I say, rolling my eyes. "We're almost there, and then we can go our separate ways—"

At that instant, a *boom* rocks the area, rippling through the air with a blast. The sound of it splits reality in half, evaporating laughter around us.

For what feels like infinity, time moves in slow motion without gravity.

There's a slant to Henry's face as I'm thrown backward, my hands flinging out in front of me. Vaguely, I hear glass shattering from every window in the building across the street. Flames grasp us inside the painful heat of its fist. Fire and smoke collapse all sight of the world as I know it until it's completely blown dark, like a candle extinguishing in the night.

Chapter Five

South of France, Present day

I'm eating lentils out of a can as I circle the greenhouse, and unfortunately, I am not alone.

The chicken trails behind me, its head curiously bobbing in various directions. A slush of soil is underfoot as I assess the structure. The red-brick foundation appears strong beneath the greenhouse, and while the glass is filthy, I can only see two spots that need repair. A lattice of vines scales around all sides, climbing into an *S* shape along the back. Dropping my spoon into the now-empty can, I set it aside and kneel at a corner. Examining closely, I see a large crack across two panels. Each glass pane is wide enough for me to fit through if I squeeze. The two panes needing repair border the surrounding metal frame, and with cracks in both, much of the cool outside air is getting in. Tapping a finger gently against the glass, it seems mostly sturdy. Probably able to withstand a storm if it's been here long. Tentatively pulling the door open, I go inside. Giving a very convincing impression of insouciance, the bird follows me in with clucks and chitters.

Inside smells of damp earth and mulch. Time tangles itself in the form of roots and weeds. The ground is still alive despite its decaying shelter. Mildew and dead leaves curl into the corners of the greenhouse. The glass is even dirtier than it appeared from outside. I tilt my neck to stare up at the belly of its gable roof, a suffusion of rain and gray morning light. I blink a few times, looking around with a sigh at the scattering of dried-out plants. I imagine early mornings in this place, with flowers of all colors blooming, their leaves unfurling through the seasons in the humid air of the greenhouse. Part of me itches to sweep its floor clean and scrub every bit of glass. I'd always grown up in cities, yet I find myself lost in what could be possible in the countryside. But I'm not here to make this place a home. I'm here for reasons greater than myself.

Turning my back on all of it, I retreat outside and close the door. My legs stride back up the slope toward the cottage. Upon entering, I shut the door swiftly and check every window before the chicken can find a way to sneak its way in. Washing my hands in the kitchen sink, I watch it wander and pluck at the ground outside. It seems to never go much further than the yard. Not even to the pier that overlooks the blue-green pond beyond the greenhouse. I don't even know where the chicken came from or where it's supposed to be. I only know it's not here.

The faucet handle creaks as I shut off the water, which I'd recently figured out was because the cottage had direct access to a nearby well. In the two weeks since I arrived, I have enough to get by, even if it's bare of much beyond the necessities. The kitchen is now well-stocked, along with the gas stove finally working after I purchased extra propane. I'd spent days emptying rooms, scrubbing floorboards, and frightening off bugs with my shrieks of surprise.

Drying my hands against the front of my pants, I take the half-dozen steps to the front room. Kneeling on the floor at eye level, I search until I see it: a small flaw in the wood, a half-inch taller than its surroundings. Taking out my knife from my back pocket, I use the flat edge to raise it at the corner. Dipping my hand into the dark below, my fingertips graze the rough ground until they meet the shape of a small bag. Lightly, I pull it out into the open. Its casing is a black sheen of fireproof material that reflects light streaming in from the kitchen window. Unzipping the bag, I hold the device in the palm of my hand. Emotions swell like a current, dragging me through its deep trenches. I am holding onto information that could kill me—nearly did kill me in London—with an undeniable helplessness that I'm wasting time here. That I should be doing more. On it are thousands of encrypted files: contacts, videos, and other media, including correspondence, and evidence of accomplices complicit in a dangerous crime syndicate who call themselves Tatrialny. Criminals who arrived from the west and settled in parts of eastern Europe. For years, they have trafficked and exploited women and children by using their suffering as nothing more than cruel leverage for financial gain. It is a war based on the profit of human lives.

Anger ignites high and tight in my chest. I have seen the roster of names of those who stand to benefit from Tatrialny's crimes around the world: presidents, members of parliament, congressmen, American politicians. I had seen firsthand what people were willing to do to those who threatened their profit margins or their public reputation. I had scars borne from learning it the hard way. I would need to get the device to the right person—but who the hell can I trust? How do I convince them to believe me if I'm the one who ran away after Emerson died?

Until that time came, I would keep it safe. I'm placing it back underneath the floorboards when suddenly, I hear a *thwack* of wood.

I freeze. A deep thudding sound seems to come from one of the back rooms. I don't wait for a third *thud* before I stand abruptly, gripping my knife. Unease is a brush stroke painting itself over my skin as I back up against the wall. Someone could have broken in without me realizing. Fear and adrenaline pour into my veins like ice water. *I don't want to die I don't want to die I don't want to die.* Violent and disturbing scenarios intrusively pierce my mind, and I almost lose my nerve to do anything beyond freeze. I could die here, today, two minutes from now, or five.

I think of Warsaw, of London, of bombs and knives and men, and remind myself that I have been through worse. After everything that has happened to me, I don't want to cower here in the corner, waiting for death to find me. With a tentative and trembling step, I move forward. Down the hall. Into the pressing walls of a cottage where my life will surely end, I think. There's been no sound for minutes now, and I can't decide if silence is worse. I raise my knife, the hilt of it firm in my grip. As I hesitantly stand at the doorframe, a roving shadow twines across the floor. I bite back a scream at first, then, when I realize it's only the face of a horse sticking its head through the open window, I lower my knife with a heavy dose of consternation. With its jaw affectionately slack, I swear it gives me a grin.

"This is absurd," I say, grimacing at the long bridge of the horse's nose staring down at me from a great height. "Do none of you have somewhere else to be?"

I never had a pet growing up; animals are foreign beings to me. Something that exists in films and books. What the hell am I supposed to do with this smiling beast?

A screech rings in the cool air of the afternoon, splitting my attention at the seams. I hurtle through the hall and toward the kitchen window as I try to figure out where the sound is coming from.

It's the chicken, or at least, what I think resembles a noise that can only come from this kind of bird.

"What the fuck, what *now*?" My eyes search frantically. "Are you both trying to get me killed?"

There—in the near distance, I can see a small, flailing shadow. The chicken appears anchored to something, with only one wing thrashing in the air. While the area is fairly remote and private, anyone could hear this sound and come to investigate. This chicken could put me at risk with its screaming. The last thing I need is someone coming here to investigate. Running out the door, I'm out of breath by the time I reach it. One of its wings is caught in the metal mouth of a trap. I hiss with surprise at the blood.

"I don't—what do I—" I choke out helplessly. The bird remains firmly stuck, and I recognize the whimpering cries in its throat as a universal sound of pain. It takes me out of my botheration, out of my discontent. I drop my knees to the ground to get a closer look. It's a spring-based trap, with a chain tethering to a pole deeply entrenched in the ground. The chain clangs and chimes as the bird tries to pull away. I can't get a firm hold. With the animal moving around so much, using my own hands is out of the question. I rush back toward the greenhouse and grab a rusted shovel, running back as fast as I can.

I wedge the shovel into the small space between the trap's teeth, using it as a lever. It's metal on metal, and the tip of the shovel slips out with a clank. A mournful, feeble sound escapes the hen, but I think it understands I'm trying. Grunting, I push the shovel against the trap to pry it apart, this time pressing hard into the footstep to get a better fit inside the metal claws. It works. I hold it open until the wing is all the way out. The trap falls over on its side at my release with a violent snapping sound, and I can see drops of blood along the inner edge of its teeth. The hen flutters far from the trap's reach, though a little unsteadily. It's quiet now. After a few unsuccessful attempts to walk away, it decides to sit where it is in the high grass. My chest heaves from the adrenaline and exertion.

The wing that had been trapped is now bent unevenly. I imagine it must be in a great deal of pain. Glancing back at the cottage, the horse neighs, its large form still looming in the frame of the back window. The field and roads are empty, and I return my attention to the chicken. What if it walks into the road, disoriented, because it needed my help? What if I'm what stands between it and living to see another day?

"I'm going to pick you up now," I announce. With caution, I begin to lean down. "If you think of taking a bite, please remember I saved you."

Nonplussed, the chicken makes small chittering sounds but is largely immobile. Cupping my hands, I lift the bird from its underbelly as gently as possible. It does not protest. With ungainly form, I pull out the key to the car from my front pocket as I carry it under one arm. Unlocking the door, I place it in the front passenger seat. I quickly return to the cottage and grab the smaller leather bag with most of the money and sling it over my shoulder. Locking the windows and the front door, I return to the car. Once I buckle up, I turn toward the chicken that is nestling quietly in the seat beside me.

"If this gets me killed, I'm turning you into lunch," I warn. It squawks dramatically in response. I start the car and reverse out of the drive, dust and dirt flying up in my rearview. I monitor the rearview mirror for a few miles to make sure I'm not being followed, though I must not value my life much, given what I decide to do next.

Chapter Six

To my luck, I find a vet is directly next to a wine shop, and both are open. By the time I carry the bird through the office door, it's mid-afternoon. I am a sweaty, disheveled mess. The office is quiet with the exception of the chicken's distress as I try to contain it in my arms. Modest lime-wash walls greet us, yet the receptionist refuses to. Her fingers pause at the keyboard as I step up to the counter. With streaks of coppery hair pulled back in a low ponytail, the woman gives me a bland expression.

"Pardon me, but is there a vet here? It needs medical attention," I tell her, lifting the chicken in my arms as I try to avoid further injuring her. The bird gives a low whine of dissatisfaction, reminding me of three-wheeled vehicles in Thailand's bustling streets—*tuk, tuk, tuk.* The woman gives me two slow blinks in reply, eyes moving between me, then the chicken, then back again.

The French are either more taciturn than Londoners, or no one understands my English.

An interior door flies open. A haste of curls and a flash of a smile come striding into the room. A woman in a white coat greets me warmly, then fixes her attention on the chicken with a wide, sympathetic smile and a sense of authority. I do hope she's the one in charge.

"Bienvenue! Viens avec moi."

With a wave of her clipboard, this new woman waves me to follow her, which I do, strolling awkwardly with the chicken at my hip. She shuffles me into a room with exactly one steel table, folded up from the wall, and a computer desk.

"Do you speak English?" I ask as she takes a seat at the computer.

"Yes, of course," she says, smiling.

"I was beginning to think I was the only one in this town," I say with relief.

"Mostly true," she tells me with a laugh. "I'm Delphine, the vétérinaire. And who is this?"

"A stray, I think? I'm not really sure."

"Do you mind if I get a bit closer?" she asks, gesturing to the table.

I nod and lean toward the table. The chicken starts to rustle more forcefully in my arms as I place it on the metal surface. Without touching the injury, Delphine assesses and points a finger along the curve of the injured wing. "What happened to the wing?"

"It's been hanging around outside the house since I arrived a few weeks ago and was there when—" I'm incredibly bad at this part where I'm meant to keep my mouth shut, I realize, "—it got caught in a metal trap," I finish.

"Hold onto her, please," she says, reaching behind her into a cabinet to pull out a pair of gloves.

"I was able to get it free without damaging it more, but it took several minutes," I add.

"Those things are *horrible*," says Delphine, the vowel clipping at the end with disgust. "The suffering they cause animals is indecent. Her pain is unnecessary."

"How can you tell it's a she?"

"The rounded feathers indicate it's a hen," she comments, indicating its back as she speaks. "If it's a male, they'll be more pointed. *Aussi*, the color pattern." Gently releasing the drooping wing, Delphine straightens with a sigh.

"I will need to cleanse the wound and determine if it is broken. She will receive some medicine to help her stay still while I scan the wing. You were right to bring her here as quickly as you did."

Delphine coos to the hen, and its head perks up with interest. "I'll return shortly," she says. The bird only mildly protests when Delphine picks it up.

The soft closing of the door leaves me alone in the exam room. An increasing awareness of my own dismay balloons. Something close to panic sticks to the roof of my mouth. Am I actually insane? What if I jeopardize my own safety because I feel bad for a hen? Was it worth the risk of exposure to come here, simply to relieve myself of guilt?

Not long after she'd left does Delphine return, both hands wrapping gently around the hen. There's a scratching sound of its claws against the metal as Delphine sets it on the folded-out table. The hen's eyes are wide and wild as if it doesn't understand why it was brought here. Both its wings are covered in a beige bandage that's also wrapped around its entire body. It sways, almost drunk-like, held together with medical tape.

"The hen is lucky. I'm confident it's merely a sprain," says Delphine, running a hand over its head affectionately. "I administered pain medication and cleaned the wound to minimize infection." She begins typing on the computer and glances at me between keys.

"Have you been here long?"

"Not long," I tell her. "I'm fixing a cottage for a distant family member who passed away." I'd already prepared to keep the basic facts of my story true, since leaning on that will lend a certain veracity to my presence here. The nightmare scenario would be getting caught later by saying the wrong thing.

"Oh!" Delphine glances up at me from her screen with a quick, bright smile. She turns back to typing. "That abandoned place outside of town? The one with the beautiful greenhouse?"

"Sounds like the one," I say with a tight-lipped smile. Later, I can lament about the scale of this town. I should be careful about being watched in a village this small. "Not sure how long I'll be here."

She's retrieving a few items in a lower cabinet, her back facing me. I'm suddenly nervous. I can't see what she's doing with her hands.

"A shame," comments Delphine. When she turns, I let out a breath to see a paper bag in her hands. "It's so nice to practice with someone who isn't my *lingo* app. Voilà!"

Handing me a small bag, it's lightweight, and I can hear a rattle of pills in a bottle. Peeking inside, I see bandages and a blue prescription bottle. The instructions are in French. Great.

"I've given you an analgesic you can give for the next few days," Delphine instructs. "It will help with the pain while the wing heals."

I nod, awkwardly reaching to retrieve the hen. It appears to be sleeping upright, then I realize it's probably high as a kite. Opening the door for me, Delphine waits for me to walk through. Between the bird and the bag, I've got my hands full.

"Keep the wound clean, and continue to wrap her wing for the next four weeks," she instructs. "She'll be fine with time. Will you give her a name?"

"I'm not going to—" I begin, but I know the less I say, the better. "It's a good suggestion."

"An animal chooses its name," says Delphine as if we're agreeing on the weather. "It will take time." She points toward the reception and hands me a slip of paper. "Give this to Brigitte, and she'll accept your payment."

"All right," I say, trying to manage everything I'm carrying. "Thank you for today."

"*C'est pas grave—*" she says with a wide smile again. "It was no problem. I do this for the animals."

Unsure of how else to end the interaction, I begin walking toward the desk where Brigitte's stoic expression awaits me.

"I didn't catch your name—" Delphine's words hang in the air behind me.

"Nora." I turn, lying smoothly. At least I'd prepared myself for that.

"*D'accord*," says Delphine, her attention already half-distracted as she reads through something on her clipboard. "Please don't hesitate to come back if you need anything else. See you next time, Nora!" She disappears through the door toward the hallway. I pay Brigitte, get the animal into the car, and drive away.

If I'm lucky, I will never see either of them again.

Chapter Seven

Warsaw, Poland, Six months earlier

Consciousness throbs behind my eyes and grips me by the shoulders. I resist the slow and weary roar of its demand. The air smells of burnt metal. It feels like something is missing. Distantly, I register someone shouting or whispering, I'm not really sure. I only know I want to go back to sleep. When did I go to sleep?

"Amara? Please answer me. Amara?"

Time, I slowly realize. I'm missing time.

Concrete is uncomfortable beneath me. When I move my arm, my skin drags across shards of something sharp. There's a plaintive moan, and it takes me several moments to understand that the sound is coming from me.

"You're okay, you're okay." That voice is familiar. "Can you open your eyes?"

"Leave me alone," I grumble.

My head is pounding like a handful of rocks shaken loose in a jar. Thoughts begin to connect me to pain in my body, and I groan, attempting to push myself up from a supine position. Clarity comes in the form of a nightmare with the burn of smoke. My eyes flutter open to the sky above me, blackened and bare branches coming into focus.

Henry is holding my face with his hands, forcing me to look at him. A line pinches between his brows, and there's a slash of red across his cheek.

"What happened?" I ask groggily.

"A bomb went off," he says. "Wait—Let me help you."

My efforts to brush him off are futile since I'm fighting against the invisible current of disorientation. I attempt to sit up straight, but everything hurts. Wincing, I reach up to push hair out of my face. My hand comes back painted in blood.

"I'm bleeding," I say with dismay.

Henry is kneeling beside me. The same dark red from his cheek is also streaked across his forearm.

"You're bleeding, too," I tell him shakily.

"Can you sit up?" he asks. "Does anything feel broken?"

"Henry, did you hear me?" I ask. He's still not meeting my eyes, so I impatiently draw his attention with a finger pointing at his arm. "You have blood on you."

"I know," he says. "It's not mine."

The aftermath is the air and on my tongue, tasting of acrid smoke and something metallic. Like burnt almonds. Looking down the block, its fresh wounds are a scene from hell; gone is the park and the sidewalk we'd taken to the edge of this intersection. Smoke plumes in the air little more than 50 meters away, set against a twilight sky. I feel the sting of glass beneath my palms. Every surface appears covered in soot and glass and death. I feel sick.

"Amara, we need to go," says Henry with urgency in his voice. "Can you walk?"

"I think so." When I attempt to push myself off the ground, a cry rattles out, and I collapse at the sudden, sharp pain in my calf.

"I'll carry you," he says, the words rushing out.

"The park," I croak weakly. "The children. What happened?"

He doesn't answer, only scoops me below my knees and behind my shoulders in one swift breath. I cry out, but the sharpness subsides when he begins walking. There isn't only mayhem during a bomb, I realize, but immediately after. The deafening silence is mayhem, too. Sirens of emergency vehicles ring in the distance,

Henry's arms are firm beneath my body, tense from the shock. A hollow, throbbing pain sits painfully behind my eyes, and I close them for relief. I'm suddenly very tired.

"Stay with me," Henry speaks clearly through the rubble of my consciousness. "We both probably have a concussion."

"But you're so irritating," I tell him, though my petulance is undermined when my head leans to rest on his shoulder.

"That's right, keep talking." His pace is smooth as he crosses the street, and he throws a quick glance over his shoulder. "What else?"

I was so close to him I could hear his racing heartbeat. His shirt smelled of burnt and terrible things.

"You spend too much money on clothes," I tell him as I force myself to open my eyes.

"How'd you make that?"

"You never wear the same shirt twice."

"Pay attention to what I wear, do you?" he asks, peering down to give a pointed look.

"If your arrogance was a tie, I think its best use would be to strangle you."

"I'm glad to see your sense of humor is still intact," he says, and he sounds like he means it.

I bite back a grimace when he steps off the sidewalk. The further we are from the blast site, the less residue there is. But there's panic, too. People are either running toward it or staring in its direction. Strangers are in shock, phones to their ears, calling for help or their loved ones. Thoughts twist out of reach, incomprehensible.

"We need to debrief Emerson as soon as possible and take a look at your injuries." He looks down at me in his arms. "Not necessarily in that order."

"The hotel should be able to call for one," I say, trying to catch up through my mental fog. "We can call Emerson first."

"Doctor first," he corrects. "Your ankle might be broken. Then Emerson."

Something about the way he says Emerson's name catches my attention.

"What about Emerson?" I ask, my eyes hovering open. "What aren't you saying?"

We're on the street with the hotel within sight, its lobby and floor-to-ceiling windows bright against a darkening sky. I can see Henry clenching his jaw.

"The same day we're set to review investigative information about Tatrialny, a bomb goes off. I think we were followed."

"Tatrialny?" I ask with puzzlement. "But who would know where I was staying—"

"Don't—" He says, quickly interrupting. "Wait until we're in the room."

I study the reserve of his expression as we enter the lobby.

"Okay," I whisper, for once without argument, and lean my head to rest against the wall of his chest. Henry asks them to call a doctor who can come to the room.

"314," I say before he can ask.

In my mind's eye, I still see the twin girls in their dresses, sisters who had run toward the swings, giggling. Fatigue pulls on my lids as if they are shutters, reality suddenly a heavy burden to carry.

Chapter Eight

South of France, Present day

Winter settles onto the landscape with the alacrity of sunny hillsides and frost that claws for life toward the cold moon each night. After eight weeks of living in the cottage, it was finally beginning to resemble a livable place.

Only after traveling to the French-Italian border for supplies and weeks of cleaning did I finally feel like maybe I could survive. I take stock of my resources every day: two powerful solar panels, firewood stacks, a few pieces of antique-looking furniture, a decent mattress for the room I sleep in, and, crucially, a French–English dictionary. Since arriving, I had begun to resent the impotence of my own incomprehension. It was like getting around with a blindfold by sheer fact that I couldn't read street signs or labels on anything. Having a dictionary would at least give me a leg up on understanding the basics.

As I heat a kettle for tea, I pull my cardigan tighter against me for warmth. Through the picture window above the sink, the sun begins its slow dip toward the edge of the countryside, glinting over the greenhouse. Both solar panels sit off to the side, like mirrors preening, their faces tipping up toward the sky's gloam. A faint pink hue of sky leaves its handprint on the glass of the greenhouse as the sun sets on the horizon. After cleaning the cloudy haze off each and every pane of glass, the interior became visible. I had begun to plant seeds with a kind of cautious comfort and reserve. White peonies, herbs, vegetables, and fruits in various containers. Every morning was time I spent watering every slight dip in the soil, waiting for something to spring up green. I need no reminder that I might need to leave it at any moment. I'm not sure I could explain to myself why I was doing it in the first place—wanting to grow things, thinking I'd be around long enough to watch them bloom.

Unfortunately, the hen follows me everywhere I go, especially now that both its wings have finally healed. Most mornings, it even trails after me when I walk to the pond behind the greenhouse. The dock sits above the glassy, incorporeal water, catching every breeze and leaf in its rippling surface. It is only a matter of steps before I hear a rustle of grass beneath its feet as it trods close by. The horse, too, continues to show up in the back bedroom window, its large nose periodically rattling against the glass for attention. My nervous agitation leads me to redirect it to an empty metal bin with a bundle of carrots, just to make it stop. It's my misfortune that it mistakes my bid as an act of generosity. Now I find myself saddled with *two* unwelcome beasts.

As the kettle boils, I step into the bedroom and grab an extra throw for sitting in front of the fire. As another winter evening descends upon the cottage in the shape of bitter winds, I return to the front room. It's mostly bare, with only a thrifted chaise, a wooden side table, and a basket large enough for the hen. The basket, like the carrots, had not been an invitation but rather a cheap bribe. A way to avoid having the bird think it was welcome to sit with me. Eyeing her now, I sit in the chaise. The bird tucks herself into an expanse of wool and wicker, clearly at peace with its lot in life.

I tell myself I'll put her back outside as soon as winter is over. Chickens are supposed to be farm animals, not domesticated pets. The subject in question is facing the direction of the fireplace, her eyes hovering at half-mast until, a few moments later, they close with satisfaction and sleep.

Taking a sip of my tea, I reach for the battered copy of the dictionary, crack open its spine, and pick back up at the *b's*. Settling in for the night, I practice aloud.

"*Un boulanger,*" I read. "Baker. *La boulangerie*, a bakery." I think of warm, fresh bread and sugar-dusted pastries.

The day's slow descent into evening bathes the cottage in semi-darkness. Logs crackle in the fireplace. In the softness of the basket, the hen continues to snooze. It's a stage set for relaxation, yet I find myself caught in the teeth of restlessness. I set the dictionary facedown in my lap. Looking at the piano, I think of London, of home. A suffusion of winter's light brings with it a sense of sorrow. The tightness in my chest is bound inside me so firmly it puts knots behind my ribcage.

Out the window, the brutal cold presses against the glass. France's rolling landscape is proof that this place is as enduring as time itself.

There is history in the hills, the wood grain of the cottage, the olive groves. They were here long before me, and will outlast me long after I'm gone. To contend with being here is to know my own mortality. I might have come here for the sake of survival, but there's a part of me that maybe belongs here more than anywhere else. For now, I exist outside the orbit of reality. I exist in a cocoon of sheer, stupid luck. It can run out at any time.

***

By the second week of February, ice crystals cling to branches as closely as boredom does to me. Unless on a supply run, I don't stray far from the cottage. Despite the low temperatures, I'm restless enough to get outside. My breath clouds in front of me like a plume of smoke. Picking up a small shovel in the yard, I make my way down the slope toward the greenhouse. Although it's a bright afternoon, it's colder in the shade. I bask in the apricity of the sunlight, its warmth pleasing against the icy pinch in my cheeks. I've nearly taken a step before I jerk back, catching myself in time to avoid tripping over the hen. It's been constantly at my feet, proving I'm not the only one going stir crazy.

"What's wrong with you?" I demand. I place a hand at the waist of my coat while my other hand chastises her with the shovel. "Did you get into the blueberries again? Did you not learn your lesson last time?"

Its gaze is fixed curiously on something behind me. I turn with panic, which quickly sours into annoyance. A small kitten sits at a small distance away, scrutinizing us.

"For fuck's sake," I groan in exasperation. "Is there nowhere else for any of you to be?"

The kitten perks up at my voice, its grey spotted ears forming two tiny triangles of eagerness. It's too young to be elegant and is a little clumsy when it makes its way in my direction. It weaves in a figure eight around my ankles, and the hen chitters at a safe distance as she closely monitors the situation. I glance down at the kitten with a narrow look.

"You're all a menace to society, do you know that?"

With an impervious stance, it peers up at me with eyes that are a startling blue. With slow blinks, it watches me with the patient wisdom of an ancient being that is also asking me to pity it. The hen has lost interest, deciding to pluck at the ground instead.

"Where the hell am I supposed to put all of you?"

I had intended for my tone to be stern, though it comes out more resigned than I had planned. It sounds less like an accusation and more like a question, which is ridiculous considering that I'm the one in charge around here.

Putting the garden shovel in my back pocket, I kneel and move slowly, not wanting to scare it off or have it bolt toward the road. The kitten watches me closely as I pull out a handful of berries. I'd made a habit of keeping some in my coat pocket for the hen, but too many make her sick. Offering one now to the kitten, it sniffs at my hand a few times before eating it in two bites. Placing a second berry in the middle of my palm, it's less hesitant and doesn't resist when I gently pick it up.

Now, at eye level, I peer into its eyes.

"I should start charging a fee if this place is going to become an overrun hotel," I mutter.

The kitten peers, almost forlornly, with its round, blue eyes. The hen is ignoring the entire exchange, wandering nonchalantly toward the greenhouse. It's almost not worth it to make declarations of where they belong; that it's not here, not with me. How has that worked out for me so far?

The kitten squirms in my hand, and I tuck it softly beneath my arm. Its mewling is the final straw.

"Fine," I relent with a sigh. It doesn't object or try to escape my hold. Pulling the shovel from my back pocket, I turn back to the greenhouse. In the fold of quiet thought, a poem begins to spread out in the space. The cat pushes the top of its head into my chest, bullying me with its affection.

"I was left behind with the immensity of existing things."

Am I the one who was left behind, or have I left behind a world that will forget about me? I am surrounded by nothing that resembles my life from before. Against me, the kitten burrows into my jacket for warmth. Its ears are so new, so tiny, I feel a protective squeeze inside my chest at how vulnerable it is. In the freezing temperature I know I cannot ignore this small creature. It may not be caught in the teeth of a trap, but it, too, is caught in the snares of a harsh and bitter reality where it will easily be forgotten if I do nothing. It could grow into its strength and its instincts. Maybe this could be the one good thing I did; maybe I could make sure there was one less being in the world that wasn't left behind.

"You caught me in a sentimental moment," I tell it, letting out a sigh. I think of the line again from the poem, and Czesław Miłosz, who'd written it long before I'd been born. "If I keep you, you should have a name. You look like an Esse to me," I murmur, handing it another berry.

A voice behind me asks, "Who is Esse?"

I choke back a scream in surprise. Spinning in the direction of the voice, my hand grips the metal shovel like a weapon in my fist to face them.

Chapter Nine

Warsaw, Poland

In the cool, quiet room of the hotel, my heart beats faster at the sight of a suture kit. A doctor, someone Henry said he'd worked with before on assignment, is retrieving belongings from a medical bag. First, a small pair of scissors, then a syringe, followed by a small glass bottle of liquid and a handful of long threads—a never-ending display of items to either treat me or torture me. Henry leans against a wall at the far end of the hotel room, a leg crossed loosely over an ankle behind the doctor. He looks down the slim shape of his nose at the doctor as if the man here to help me is the problem.

"Always bloody hovering," I mutter under my breath.

Henry's eyes slide away from the doctor's syringe to me.

"I can hear you."

"I meant you to."

The doctor is a man with silver hair that matches the frames of his glasses, which refract from a lone lamp nearby. Evening sets its burnt orange wash on the film of chaos a kilometer away. Though there isn't much light left in the day, the doctor makes quick work of pushing the curtains apart to let in as much natural light as possible.

At my trepidation at the sight of the needle in his hand, he gives me a patient smile.

"I've been doing this for many years," he says, his words outlining the shape of an accent and a smile, "and the only complaints I've heard are from my wife, who says I work too much."

I'm so nervous that a puff of laughter escapes. Swallowing, I fixate on the air vent just above the full-length mirror, a current of cool air mixing with the stagnation in the room. Gently but swiftly, the doctor cleans the skin at my hairline with a medical-grade disinfecting wipe. The bleeding has finally stopped, and I feel a pinch as he begins to numb the area. When the air vent suddenly goes quiet, it's as if a pause button has been pressed. The abrupt silence in the room makes me realize how loud my ears are ringing. Tossing the cleansing wipe in the trash bin, he leans in with the thread and needle.

"You don't need to worry," offers Henry without solicitation.

I flinch as the doctor pulls the thread upward for the first stitch.

"Leave it to a man for impeccable timing," I say. When the doctor quirks a brow, I clear my throat and say in Polish, "Not you, I'm sorry. You have excellent timing."

"You speak very well," he replies in Polish with surprise. "Where did you learn?"

"I had a language tutor growing up." My mouth clamps shut as soon as I feel a tugging on the skin along my hairline. Even with the numbing, I can still feel the sensation, and it scoops out all the bravado I thought I'd had. Closing both eyes, I focus on my breathing. Talking distracts me, so I keep going. "I continued studying in university, including literary Eastern European writers who published after the Second World War."

"Very impressive," he says kindly. "You must know quite a lot about our culture then. How hard it was for our city."

This close to him, I can see the grooves in his forehead as he focuses on stitching, and the soft crinkle of faint lines around his eyes. He could be the age of my father, if I knew who that was.

"The first time I heard about how the Germans destroyed the city during the Warsaw Uprising, I was so terribly sad about it I stayed in my room for a week," I tell him softly. "I didn't understand how no one had stopped this terrible thing from happening. When I told my mother I wanted to attend the annual Day of Remembrance, my mother said we could go on one condition: She asked whether my sadness was useful, or if it was sadness masquerading as pity. If I could answer her honestly that it was the first, not the second, then she would take me."

A ghost of a smile spreads across the doctor's face as he makes a small knot with the thread.

"Your mother sounds like a very wise woman." He snips in the air just out of my line of vision, reviewing his handiwork along my forehead. "What happened?"

"I wanted to honor Warsaw in the way that Warsaw prefers to," I reply, not wanting to correct him that my mother passed away. "We came to the capital and joined the city in lighting red flares and pausing for a moment of silence while the sirens sounded. It changed my life."

Goosebumps scatter across my arms as I remember it; the red light illuminating between my mother's hands, the stripes of Polish flags waving. It wasn't only a curtain of harmless smoke drifting overhead, blotting out the sky; it was also pride to have been born in a place where the people have persevered through the test of time with such strength that they once rebuilt themselves from the rubble of destruction. The echo of more recent destruction is not far from where we sit now, and something resembling guilt and heartache nearly spills out. I swallow them whole.

"I can tell you understand the history." The doctor places a gentle hand on my arm. "The city will have to heal again after today, too."

"Mind if I take a look?" Asks Henry, the man who reliably can ruin A Moment.

"Ignore him," I tell the doctor, casting a look of irritation at Henry. "Why don't you make yourself useful? I could use some water."

"I live to serve," Henry says, going to the fridge. He places a bottle of water in my hand.

After returning the sharper items to his kit, the doctor wraps all of his remaining materials in the tan, leather medical bag. I drink the ice-cold water in my hand, soothing my dry, scratchy throat. I down nearly the entire thing.

The doctor rests a hand on my shoulder.

"Nine stitches, very minor. Drink more water; you must hydrate as much as possible." He hands me a small pill bottle with a dozen or so capsules. "Take twice a day for pain, and stay off the ankle. It's a sprain that will heal fine. You are very lucky," he says sadly.

The doctor turns, giving Henry a polite nod before walking out the door of the hotel room. Then, it's only Henry and me in a silent standoff.

"I'm trained for emergencies, you know," says Henry. "I lead on-site emergency medical contingencies. I'm entirely capable."

"I agree that you are very capable," I say, speaking slowly so he doesn't misunderstand me, "of being insufferable."

Ignoring me, Henry points to the bottle in my hand. "Looks like he gave you the good stuff."

"For pain. Your absence would give me a jump start." I proffer my spite with a saccharine smile.

When a small vibration sounds from where Henry is standing, he reaches inside his jacket pocket and pushes off the wall. Pulling up a chair to the edge of the bed where I'm sitting, he puts his phone on speaker.

"Emerson," Henry answers on the second ring. "Amara and I are both here."

"Hi, Emerson," I say, wincing as I adjust to a slightly more upright sitting position. Henry moves to place a pillow behind me. I swat him away.

"Amara," Emerson replies, his voice edging with worry. "I'm glad to hear you're all right. I have my reservations about pulling you into this investigation beyond my initial request, however..."

"Sir," Henry interjects. "I think she should be read in. The fact that she speaks Polish will be an asset given the intel."

"I agree," Emerson agrees. "Given the circumstances, we need to jump in fairly quickly here, then—in immediate effect, your security clearance has been raised due to the circumstances."

"Understood, sir," I say.

"You are being thrust into an investigation that has been ongoing for the better part of a year," he says, sounding strained. "Organized crime is the biggest threat to the UK, but it is also a threat to the European continent. Agent Clark has been actively tracking a syndicate called Tatrialny. In the hierarchy of their functions, Roman Górski is the decision-maker. He's also the most visible player. Tatrialny's illegal imports and exports operate in the bounds of official channels that are sensitive in nature, and our aim is to disrupt that."

"What kind of products?" I ask, mentally enumerating the possibilities. "Are we talking about fentanyl-laced pills, illegal trade of animals—"

"Not drugs," says Henry, a hesitant pause so small I almost think I've made it up, except his voice is wound tight like a rope coiling around his throat. "Children."

"Nearly all of whom come from foster care," adds Emerson grimly. He may know about my upbringing on a personal level, but he's the chief of MI6 speaking now. "Tatrialny believes it minimizes risk for their operations if they utilize persons who won't trigger an immediate report of them missing."

My breath catches like needles in my ribcage. Thoughts of my childhood are a flashbulb illuminating every thought of *could have been*, and *what if* I've ever had. I don't ask the obvious question of why someone would do something so awful, because I already know: For every bit of innocence in the world, there's always someone hunting to exploit it.

"...We've been tracking parts of Western and Eastern Europe with elevated activity," Emerson is saying. "Thanks to Agent Clark, we have intel about tech that contains Tatrialny's blueprint to carry out a complex political strategy intended to infiltrate governments all over the world to expand their operations. This strategy could involve bullying members of parliament for votes or blackmail."

"The bomb points to blackmail," says Henry. He looks away from me, and there's something careful about his expression.

Emerson continues. "Among the elected officials we suspect are associated with Tatrialny, there are whispers of a plan to push legislation that will provide loopholes to decriminalize future convicted traffickers, ultimately making it a benign crime with a lower rate of sentencing."

"How many countries that we know of have elected officials associated with this group?" My tongue unglues from the roof of my mouth, and my legal mind goes to work. "How high does their status go?"

"That's the question we need to find out," says Emerson.

My head swims with hypotheticals. "So it could be mayoral, parliamentary—"

"It could be anyone," Henry adds.

A thought flickers like a light as understanding dawns on me.

"The playground," I say with shock. "The bomb was intentional.

For Henry—I mean, Agent Clark?"

"It's too soon to be definitive," says Emerson. His voice sounds gruff. "The fact that you both walked away gives me pause about it being a direct attack on him. The park seems to have been the target. We need to find out why."

I'm suddenly in the murky past, standing on the sidewalk from two hours before, watching twin sisters in matching dresses, or further back, standing in a fog of red light, a cloud of grey vapor obscuring where the past ends and the present begins.

"Who knew you would be here?" Henry asks with a hint of accusation. I realize he's directing his question to me.

"Aside from Emerson? A few colleagues at the office knew some of my trip itinerary. It wasn't a secret," I tell him.

"The bombing occurred not far from your hotel," Emerson points out. "He's right to ask, though I'm not sure there's a connection."

"I understand, but isn't that a better question for Clark?" I suggest, not without an edge of defensiveness. "He's the agent who's been working on this case. Could someone have discovered the investigation?"

"Aside from Emerson, only my informant knew I was here," says Henry matter-of-factly. "When I received his call, I left straightaway after the dead letter box."

"It's in your possession?" Asks Emerson, agitation sounding through the phone.

"Yes, sir."

"Was access provided to the device?"

"Ah—no, not quite," says Henry. Maybe it's because I hardly trust him that there's something about his wince that looks too careful to be believable. "The keys for access have been kept separately, though I've been told they *are* duplicated, so they're not aware it's missing at this point yet. It's a new kind of technology, which neither of us has seen before. Without knowing what we're working with, we should be extremely careful. We may only get one shot at the information."

"This is a major asset," says Emerson, "that could confirm the full roster of names, geopolitical locations, and language in legislation that points to where the domino may fall first. That device is the entire key to this operation."

"That's why you needed me," I realize, finally catching up. "Because I can review the legal ramifications of what is possible in international court. To intercept and possibly modify the language before it's cemented into constitutions."

Just then, I hear a knock in the background on the phone and Emerson murmuring, "Tell Grace I'll be right there."

When Emerson returns to the conversation, it's a little hurried.

"Amara, take the week, and if you can come in on Monday, let's schedule a meeting first thing. Tell Tom to put you on my schedule," he says, referring to his chief of staff.

"And Clark," adds Emerson distractedly as I hear him shuffling through something, "get both of you on a flight back to London. Check with your source. See about getting visibility into the signal device."

Henry's thumb hovers over the screen of the phone.

"Yes, sir."

Without another word, the line cuts out.

"I'll work on booking a flight," says Henry, abruptly standing. There's an inscrutable look on his face. "Maybe aim for a departure in the late morning so you can get some sleep."

"If I weren't in so much pain, I would disagree with you," I say, adjusting one of the pillows more comfortably behind me.

"If you take the medication now, you'll be asleep in less than ten minutes."

"But what if I—" I swallow in fear that turns into a lump in my throat. "What if I hear it all again when I close my eyes? What if I see that little girl and I can't wake up?"

He doesn't cover me with a blanket of useless platitudes, and that, I think, might be the only redeemable thing to come out of his showing up in Warsaw.

I look down at the capsules in my palm. After another moment of hesitation, I finally toss them back. I set the empty water bottle on the nightstand, where a matchbook lies face up. It's small, with the scroll of the hotel's name on the front, and I stare at it blankly for longer than I realize until Henry begins to turn away.

My hand grabs for his arm with a mind of its own. I can think of a million things to say to him; I think he's a prick, an infuriating hassle—but truthfully, I simply don't want to be alone.

As if sensing my thoughts, he steps back toward the edge of the bed and sits. We don't say anything for several moments.

"I didn't know you spoke Polish," he says finally.

"You don't know a lot of things about me," I say. It comes out a bit more snappish than I intend.

"Seems like the medication needs a few more minutes to kick in." A curving and wry smile lifts the corner of his mouth.

I relent. "I had a tutor. My parents actually adopted me not far from here and felt it was important to remember where I came from, even growing up in America. Now that both my parents have passed away, I came here to..." A hand gestures vaguely in the air. "You know."

"Find out something about yourself?" he asks. "See what the past has to tell you?"

I begrudge him for seeing through it so clearly. Henry's eyes move over my face as if it will somehow unlock whatever puzzle he's trying to solve.

"I remember you mentioned being adopted," he remarks. "I hadn't realized they'd both passed."

I let the sting of his words pinch in my chest and tell myself, surely, the heartache will go away eventually.

"They passed a few years after I moved to London," I tell him, looking out the window. "I had hoped coming here would lead to some answers, but the woman at the children's home didn't know anything."

"Was there anything else you had wanted to see here?" he asks, leaning back on his hands.

"There's an exhibit featuring a writer I studied in uni. Manuscripts and photographs and other things."

"Anyone good I would know?"

"I wasn't aware you were literate."

His laugh is a deep rumble that vibrates through his palms, which rest on the duvet cover.

"My entire undergrad was devoted to the published work of Czeslaw Milosz," I say, by way of explanation.

His expression is thoughtful as he looks at me. "*Both your sins and good deeds will be lost in oblivion*," he recites, leaning in, a glint in his eyes.

My brows shoot up. "I wouldn't have taken you for a reader of 20th-century Polish literature."

"You find it unbelievable that I could devote myself to something as meaningful as art?" he asks with mock indignation.

I give him a flippant smile as an answer. Slipping deeper into the cushion of the bed, drowsiness begins to blur the edges of my vision. He's watching me, waiting, I think, for me to say something first.

Shadows cast into the corners of the room, but our eyes catch mid-air like a match striking. Despite how much time has passed since last fall, somehow I am once again sitting in the dark with him, his gaze capturing my breath in the air as if he has plucked it by the fingers between us.

"Why are you looking at me like that?" I ask, though it comes out like I could fall asleep mid-sentence.

"No reason."

"Liar."

A sigh. "It's just that you are..." he seems to be searching for the word.

"What am I?" As I close my eyes, curiosity hangs over a cliff with my consciousness.

"I'd say the most clever woman I've met, but I doubt you'd believe me."

"You..." I'm drifting off, the medication dragging me slowly down like a stone falling into a lake toward the bottom. "...should get out more."

Each word stretches like a band on the brink of breaking. I can't remember closing my eyes, but it's dark now. I feel Henry's hand on my arm, open and soft. I fall asleep that way, the feel of him lingering beside me.

***

Hours later, the night sky is an ink stain out the window. I lurch forward, breathing hard. Where am I?

Throwing the covers back, I wince from the pain snapping at me from my ankle. The medication must have worn off, or maybe the adrenaline ate away at it. I peer at my phone, which Henry must have placed on the nightstand, and realize I'm alone. The events of the day—the bomb, the playground, the call with Emerson—come rushing back. My eyes adjust to the dimness of the room, partially lit by the moon through the open shades. I am so parched, my throat filled with fissures and cracks like one finds in a desert. Slowly, I rise from the bed. Spotting a pair of silver crutches against the dresser near the mirror, I wonder if Henry brought them here while I slept.

Where is he?

In the far corner of the room, the bathroom light streams underneath the door. Faintly, I can hear a low voice through the wall. Grunting slightly, I raise myself on my good leg and hop-walk to the crutches. Placing one beneath my arm on the same side as my injury, I quietly take a few steps toward where the voice is coming from. It's Henry, but I can only hear his part of the conversation.

"...He knew about the devi—" His tone is hardly perceptible through the door, his voice going in and out. Layers of something secretive and hushed. "...There's no clear indication of how..."

I hover silently, trying to get closer.

"She has no insight, Antoni. The bomb was an obvious hit and could have fucking killed us, but it's safe. He seemed—exactly, yes. He knows I have it."

The crutch, which I'd been holding as I leaned closer to the door, crashes against the floor. Abruptly, Henry goes quiet on the other side. Suddenly, the bathroom door is thrown open. I blink owlishly, squinting at the bright, fluorescent lighting. My eyes adjust to my own reflection in full view of the bathroom vanity behind him, and I can see the line of new stitches braided along my temple, dark tendrils of unbrushed hair hanging loose in front of my face. The normal olive tone of my skin appears wan.

Henry is holding his phone in his left hand, the call ended, with the screen bright. He's watching me with a grave expression, as if waiting to see what I say next. He's a full head taller, so I give a stubborn lift of my chin to meet his gaze.

"Why are you whispering about the device?"

Chapter Ten

South of France, Present day

My heart hammers forcefully against my ribs. Reality swims into focus, and I loosen my grip on the shovel.

"Delphine?" I'm trying to catch my breath. "What are you doing here?"

"*Oui*, it's me," she says, studying me carefully. "You look pale. Are you all right?"

Air in my lungs releases as I let out a partially hysterical laugh, slightly high even to my own ears.

"I'm fine."

I straighten and force my posture to relax. Shifting the kitten to my other hand, my gaze meets hers. "What brings you here?"

Noticing the small cat for the first time, Delphine exclaims with enthusiasm and a clap of her hands.

"*Un petit chat!* What a precious thing." She reaches forward to pat its tiny head. Glancing at me, she asks, "She's yours?"

I look down at it in my arms. "I only found her a few minutes before you arrived."

"Ah, okay, I see. And the bird!" She exclaims as it pecks at the ground near my feet. "You decided to keep them both!"

Delphine leans down to greet the hen, and it goes to her like a long-lost friend. Its feathers ruffle avidly as she pets it on the head. Traitor.

"I can't get any of them to leave," I say with a derisive snort.

"Did I hear you say you named it... Esse?" she asks, rising to her feet.

"It's the name of a poem." I hope my nonchalant shrug is more convincing than it feels.

"Anyone I know?" she asks with a curious smile.

"A Polish one," I say vaguely.

I'm afraid at first that I've said too much. Yet after a moment of silence with only a breeze brushing against tall grass, I don't know what compels me to fill it.

"There's a horse, too, that comes by sometimes," I add, pointing in the direction of the back window of the cottage. "Dark hair, male. Mérens breed, I think? At least according to a book I read. I once made the mistake of giving it food to go away, but it keeps coming back. I'm not sure why there are so many loose animals around here. Don't they belong to someone?"

The last part comes out with a subtle note of vexation, and it occurs to me my comment might come off as insulting.

"There are, it's true," she says with a nod. "Sometimes too many. When I was a child, I would take in so many animals. I detested leaving them outside in bad weather, which would exasperate my *maman*."

"You seem like a natural," I say, meaning it, as the hen watches Delphine curiously. "Your mother must not be surprised you work with animals now."

"True," says Delphine, biting back a smile as she gestures toward the two animals. "It must also be difficult to want your solitude and yet find yourself suddenly in charge of them."

"Yes, they've really staged a *coop* of the cottage," I tell her dryly.

She gives me a confused expression, though she quickly becomes animated.

"Oh! Coop like a coup—ha!" Delphine lets out a wide, open laugh. "You really surprise me, Nora. You're funny."

"Sometimes," I say, "though usually only in foreign countries."

With a shiver from the chill in the air, I pull my jacket against me. My layer is too thin to be out here much longer. When I open my mouth to find a polite way to bow out of the interaction, Delphine beats me to it.

"I don't mean to keep you," she comments, giving a brief glance at the greenhouse and the solar generators, but turns her attention back to the hen. "I was nearby and wanted to check on your bird. It seems like its wing has healed very nicely."

"Not my bird," I correct. With a small wave in the direction of the slope up toward the cottage, I say, "I should bring this one inside from the cold. Probably see if I have milk for the cat—"

"It looks young still, maybe eight, nine weeks old," she says, peering at the kitten as it tries to burrow its head into my jacket. "A little too young still for cow's milk, but water will be okay."

"They can't drink milk?" I hadn't realized.

"A mother's milk is okay, but most cats cannot digest cow's milk very well. It's okay not to know where to be cautious with certain animals," says Delphine with a reassuring smile. "I can examine it inside if you'd like? Help you get it settled until you figure out what you would like to do?"

A sensation of needles prick along my arms at the offer. I look toward the cottage, the sky a shade of bright blue and yellow sun. Would saying no draw more attention? How far does my distrust extend to this stranger who seems genuinely concerned for the animal? I really don't want to appear like I have something to hide, and decide that if Delphine had wanted to harm me, she had the chance while I was distracted with the cat.

"Sure," I say. "I can make us tea."

"That sounds divine." Delphine's smile widens.

I lead the way up the small hill. The hen follows slowly beside me while the kitten curls over my palm. Inside, the cottage is warm with the fire I'd lit earlier. Delphine follows in, and I shut the door behind us. There's an empty box in a closet that I bring out, and as I pull out the top layer of several blankets, my eyes catch sight of the shape of the gun I keep there. Securing the latch on the closet door, I bring the box and the blanket and set the kitten gently inside, the walls of the cardboard too high for it to climb out. I hand the box to Delphine, who accepts it readily and begins to inspect the cat's fur and limbs.

"I'll start the tea," I tell her as I begin filling the kettle. I gesture with a wave to the table next to the window. "You're welcome to sit."

Grabbing a ceramic dish from the cabinet, I eye the switchblade I'd hidden next to a few plates. While water begins to boil, I pour tap water into a small dish. Delphine gently examines the kitten. She places the dish inside the box, and the cat begins to drink.

"Do you take milk or sugar with your tea?" I ask over my shoulder.

"Milk, no sugar, *merci,*" she says.

When the water is ready, I steep tea bags in two mugs and carry them over. The hen is lying in its familiar basket near the fire. Delphine has finished examining the cat and places it back inside the makeshift bed in the box. Perhaps because of the warmth or satisfaction from quenching its thirst, it seems tired enough to rest in the layers of fabric. Its blue eyes close sleepily. Taking a sip of my tea, Delphine doesn't hide her curiosity about the open layout or sparse space of the cottage. My eyes track her every movement.

"I wondered if perhaps you had left," she says. "Only as I was driving to the fish market did I notice your car as I began to pass by. I'm sorry if I startled you. Outside, before."

With a practiced air lacking concern, I say after a sip of tea, "I was only distracted by the cat."

"A cat, a chicken, a horse..." She smiles over her cup, steam floating in the air like a question mark. "Do you have names for them all?"

I laugh before I can stop myself. "Unfortunately, yes."

"Oh, please do share," she says so earnestly, I figure there's no harm in it.

"Well, you've met Esse, obviously," I tell her, pointing to the kitten in the box at my feet. "Albert is the horse, though I suspect it has an owner and shelter since I only see him intermittently."

"And what about..." Delphine drifts off with a hand gesturing to the sleeping hen in its basket.

I lower my shoulders in defeat with a heavy sigh. "Céline."

"Did you come up with that just now?" she asks with an easy laugh.

"She seems like a Céline, no?" I wrap my hands around the delicate mug to keep me warm. "Classy, yet dramatic. Has expensive taste in berries." I'd give Céline a pointed look, but the hen continues her slumber, so it'd be lost on her anyway. Turning to Delphine, I add, "You're the only one who speaks English here that I've met. Did you study somewhere?"

"I was an au pair in Seattle for a year," says Delphine. "It was after university, before I completed school to become a *vétérinaire*. Which means it was a long time ago now—" a laugh, "I haven't anyone to practice with anymore, and have forgotten a lot of colloquialisms."

"If you can say colloquialism in your non-native language, I think you're safe," I tell her with a chuckle. "So you returned after a year in California. Then what did you do?"

She leans back. "I returned to France to study in Nantes. I grew up very close to here, actually. My mother is only six kilometers away or so," she says with a finger toward the road out the window. "I always spent time with animals. Their suffering has always weighed very heavily on me. What I do gives me purpose."

"How many animals do you have?" I ask.

"Just the two kids—" Delphine glances up from her tea. "Oh, you mean pets."

A laugh surprises me when it bubbles out.

"Let's see—" She begins to enumerate on her right hand. "Two Pyrenees, one goat, one horse, and a rabbit. It's all a very delicate balance," she says seriously. "I have to make sure the dogs don't confuse the rabbit for food."

Finishing my tea, I set the cup aside. Taking the cue, Delphine rises from the chair and stretches her arms above her head.

"I should head home. Thank you again for the wonderful tea and conversation."

"You're welcome," I tell her with a polite nod.

"If you'd like, you're welcome to bring Esse to my office," she proffers, "I can run some tests, make sure she doesn't have worms at the very least."

"I might," I say. "Thank you for the offer."

Delphine reaches for the door and turns to wave as I stand in the frame. Cold air spills into the room and sweeps a chill at my ankles.

"*Au revoir*, Nora," she calls. Her keys jingle in her hand as she gets into her car. "See you soon!"

Waving goodbye, I watch her reverse out of the drive. Long after the two-door Peugeot disappears down the lane and onto the main road, I close the front door, latching the double bolt. Not trusting the cat on its own, I carry it from room to room as I check each window lock and close every shade. In the bathroom, I peer out toward the west, where dusk begins to settle its handprint in the late afternoon. Returning to the main room, I bring the box down off the table and place it next to the hen. I kneel on the floor and shift the edge of the rug slightly until I find it.

Lifting the removable floorboard, I set aside the plank of wood. Unzipping the fireproof bag, I hold the hard drive in my palm. The device is unchanged, its locking mechanism in place. Delphine's visit, the vulnerability of the device—all of it winds up my anxiety. Even with my perpetual proximity to it, it's still not enough assurance. Having it here is definitely a risk. Delphine's surprise visit leaves me feeling suddenly exposed.

Studying the hardware, I mentally map out measures I need to take. Measures I should have taken months ago. Emerson was killed for the information I'm keeping. I was responsible for that death. Every day I am alive is only a reminder of it.

Chapter Eleven

South of France, Present day

My paranoia transmutes into something akin to a phantom limb that's never forgotten. Late spring showers rinse the landscape clean. Daylight hours stretch further each day across fields and rooftops. My entire world has shrunk to the few cubic meters of the cottage, the greenhouse, and occasionally, the nearby town. I avoid perceivable routine as much as possible when I'm in town—should any watchful eyes attempt to catch me off guard—and watch over my shoulder everywhere I go. I've made sure weapons are within easy reach, hidden throughout both the greenhouse and the cottage. I inventory them weekly. It is the most consistent part of any routine I keep.

It's been a slow process, but I have finally finished repairing the greenhouse, including every broken glass pane. Seeds I had planted months ago now produce a variety of colors on my dinner plate. At first, aphids attacked my lettuce. From a used book on vegetable gardening, I learned that ladybugs could be used to control pests. Parsley, dill, tomatoes, cucumbers, and legumes sprout from soil as if they had always been here in the warmth of the greenhouse.

My pansies grow better in crates instead of the ground. Far more convenient, too, to move them around more easily.

While my world has become smaller than I ever believed it might, it has also become bigger than I'd ever imagined. Despite my best efforts, I have not been left unbothered. Albert still taps his nose against the window for attention, though he's taken to the one above the kitchen sink, where he knows he can find me more often than not. While Céline and Albert enjoy their freshly peeled carrots, Esse extravagantly eats a tin of fish I set on the kitchen floor, gradually making her way across one side of the room to the other with licks and scrapes. Delphine occasionally stops by. She brings goat's milk and corn kernels for Céline, as well as a bottle of wine for me. She never pries for information, mostly sharing anecdotes of her four-legged patients and her two-legged children, and so with each visit, my shoulders lower a little further from my ears. If it is a ruse, then my loneliness gives in to the pressure until I quell any objections. Even to the animals.

We've all grown accustomed to each other—even Esse and Céline. Céline makes preening, cooing noises when she sleeps, while Esse frequently falls asleep curled against the pillow. At first, I grumbled about Esse's tiny paws pressing into my face, but it was a dramatic performance more than anything else. The contented vibrations draw me out of heartache: I'm not completely alone. I don't want to be alone anymore.

One late afternoon, I'm inside the cottage attempting to bribe Esse. It doesn't take much—just some cat treats to bring her near enough to grab her. Protesting, she lets out a lugubrious whine. The pitch of it is full of objections to convey her distrust. Esse resentfully peers at me through her narrowing glare. Since winter, she's been much more vocal about her dissatisfaction.

"I knew it before, but you really are French, just so you know."

She lets out another dismal and dramatic yowl as I place her inside a carrier.

"Going to a vet appointment is not mistreatment," I castigate. "Five months ago, you didn't even have a home. Now you have a warm bed and a fancy bowl to drink out of every night. Think of how easy you have it."

A half hour later, I'm standing in a room at the vet's office, watching Esse purr loudly against Delphine's arm.

"She had objections about coming here," I reveal resentfully. "She only relented for the treats."

Delphine laughs and scratches under Esse's chin. "She looks good, healthy. No adverse symptoms since her booster vaccine a few months ago?"

"No reaction," I say, shaking my head. Delphine gives Esse another treat. "She's been normal, which for her means she never listens to a word I say. Are all cats like this?"

"Cats only do what cats want to do," says Delphine in a sing-song voice, smiling as Esse nibbles treats from her palm. Placing Esse gently back into the carrier, she hands it to me. She walks me back toward the front, where Brigitte turns a page from a book she's reading. Delphine is scribbling a note of something on her clipboard when she suddenly turns to look at me enthusiastically.

"Oh!" she says. "I forgot to tell you. Someone was looking for you."

Everything is bright and sharp and loud. Delphine's hands wave animatedly as she continues.

"Well—I think they were looking for you. He didn't use your name, only asked about you. Said he was a friend."

"A friend?" Fear carves through me like winter's icy and a twisting blade.

"Or..." Delphine's eyebrows knit in concentration to remember. "A colleague? Something like that."

My hands become fists as I grip the cat carrier.

"Did he say what he wanted?" The words rush out. "What did he look like?"

"He didn't say," says Delphine as she taps at her temple with a finger. "It was actually Brigitte he spoke with—"

"I need to go," I say and begin walking to the door. "I'm sorry."

"Wait, Brigitte can tell you more—" Delphine says, but I'm already gone.

Sprinting to the car, I hurry and put the cat in the passenger seat. With a quick glance behind me, I throw the car into reverse. Mud splatters against the side of the car. The town disappears in my rearview mirror as I speed to the cottage. My palms are clammy against the steering wheel. Reaching down, I search carefully until my fingertips meet the barrel of a gun. I retrieve it from the velcro bag I'd used to secure it underneath the driver's seat. With nimble hands, I check the ammo.

Six bullets.

Gravel flies up in my rearview through the last particles of daylight. There are less than 15 kilometers until I reach the cottage. I hit the gas pedal to reach it as fast as I can. I don't want to be caught there in the dark.

Chapter Twelve

By the time the cottage is within sight, my knuckles are white from clutching the steering wheel. On instinct, I drive past it to park the car a distance down the road. While I consider leaving the cat inside the car, I decide to take Esse with me. She looks curiously around as if sensing we're not far from home. I'm too morbid, afraid that if something were to happen to me, she would be in the car alone with no way to get out.

Sliding a hand under her belly, I bring her out of the carrier and set her down. The countryside sings its mournful tune as the last moments of daylight burn off in the distance. I've got a firm grip on the gun as I move briskly through the meadow behind the cottage. I take a winding route that will bring me to the bottom of the slope near the greenhouse. Esse begins to wander freely, recognizing that we're home.

Pressing up the slope, the house comes into view. Moving toward the farthest window, I glance over my shoulder to see Esse watching me. I turn back and stay out of sight as I check each window from an angle where I won't be seen.

All seems as it should: the furniture undisturbed, details as they'd been when I'd left.

Until I hear it.

Through the bedroom window facing the garden, I catch sight of a figure. I duck out of sight. Feeling lightheaded, I stand with my back against the stone. I strain to listen. Taking another peek, I see him moving through the cottage. He's making his way to the back, toward the bathroom.

The instant I hear footsteps on the tile floor, I move swiftly toward the courtyard.

Every second counts.

Every breath keeps my mind clear and focused.

The door is slightly ajar. Holding my breath, I gently ease it open as quietly as I can. With the gun steady at my thigh, I carefully enter. A fire is going, and not one I'd lit. On the countertop are two large kitchen knives, and something is soaking in the sink. A brief glance tells me Céline isn't in the basket. Worry sinks in my stomach. When the whistle of the kettle sounds, I squeeze myself against the wall and out of sight. The man strolls back to the kitchen. He hasn't noticed yet that one of the knives is missing.

I'm facing his back, unseen. He's whistling at the long side of the kitchen. *My* kitchen. Raising the gun at his back, I cock it. It makes him go suddenly still.

He slowly turns to face me, a phoenix rising out of death and ash and darkness. I gasp.

Chapter Thirteen

Warsaw, Poland

We are in a standoff, with Henry backlit. Fluorescence from the bathroom vanity glares almost as harshly as I do.

"What are you—"

"For your own safety, Amara," Henry interjects, "it's better if you don't know."

"Try again."

"You have no idea what you overheard, and—"

"Are you going to tell me who Antoni is?" I ask.

"No," he says, peering up at me, then looking away. "I can't tell you that."

"Because it's classified?"

"Telling you anything about him is exposure," he states coldly, "and that jeopardizes the entire arrangement."

"You know what also jeopardizes your arrangement? Dying in a bomb attack," I spit out. The medication is clouding my focus and would make me groggy if anger wasn't grabbing me by the shoulders. "I'm as much a part of it as you now."

"Can we sit, please?" he asks, palms facing out as a concession.

"You look as if you might faint."

"You can't stall forever."

He narrows his eyes at me as I wobble against the crutch.

"Amara, for fuck's sake. Please, will you sit?"

When I continue to refuse, he releases a heavy sigh and mutters, "You are the most stubborn—" before taking a seat on the corner of the bed. Leaning his forearms across his thighs, he drags a hand over his face.

"Are you going to tell me what you meant by, 'he knows I have it'?"

He recoils. "Jesus—is there any part you didn't hear?" As if resigning himself to something, he looks up at me with an expression so despairing it takes me by surprise.

"Someone at MI6 is working for Tatrialny," he finally says. "My informant doesn't know who it is, but he knows it's someone who is trying to get close to the investigation."

"Your informant seems to know some pretty urgent information, with the exception of the most helpful part. How do you know he's not attempting a disinformation campaign?"

Henry snorts. "He and I have a mutual interest and common goal to cease Tatrialny's operations. The intel he exchanges is not only highly sensitive but also puts his own life at risk. As do I. The only trust we have is knowing each of us risks our lives to divulge coveted intel. This is the cost of doing business."

Giving in, I sit as far from him as physically possible on the bed and set the crutch on its side between us.

"So what do you think you overheard?" he asks, turning to look at me. Despite the little amount of light in the room, his eyes shine as they catch mine.

"I think... You don't want Emerson to know about the signal-based device. Why?"

"That's the thing. I never told anyone it's a signal-based device," Henry says quietly. "I only found out myself when I received it."

"But how would Emerson know?" I ask, pressing a hand against my forehead as my head begins to throb. "That would mean that he—"

"—that he is likely a known associate with a vested interest in making it disappear. Yes," he remarks. From his shirt pocket, he retrieves something small enough to fit in the palm of his hand.

My disbelief renders me speechless as soon as I see it. Henry places it into my hand. It's black, thin, and compact, weighing almost nothing. A raised section, the shape of a crescent moon, swivels from side to side, concealing some kind of thumb pad.

"A biometrics feature," he says. "Not the only security mechanism, but the biggest obstacle so far. Pretty much impossible to falsify."

"I don't understand," I say in disbelief. The years I've known Emerson drown out all logic. "Why would Emerson protect Tatrialny? What would he have to gain?"

"Sometimes it's more about what people don't want to *lose*," Henry tells me. "Motivations can be tricky to uncover. Maybe there's something they know about him that we don't. But if it's

Emerson my informant has heard about within MI6, it would make sense why his name is being censored among the lower ranks. A relationship like that would only benefit Tatrialny. It'd be the card they'd want to hold closest to the chest."

I'm overwhelmed at the notion that this could be true. Never once have I witnessed him behave without integrity. I refuse to believe it.

"Perhaps he guessed correctly," I tell him. "Device is such an ambiguous term—"

Henry shakes his head. "He didn't only say device, he said signal. Do you know what that means?"

"I imagine you're going to tell me," I remark icily.

"Signal, too, is an ambiguous term; it's a special coded technology that could be audible or visual." Henry turns his profile to face me, the slim of his nose illuminated from the faint light of the bathroom. "Emerson didn't say *a* signal device, he said *the* signal device. There are very few of them in circulation. They're not only tricky to unlock but very special. So fucking special that Tatrialny *built* it," Henry finishes.

It sounds so much like truth that disbelief wedges a dark and unpleasant wedge into the crevice of my confidence. We sit for a long while without speaking. How do I object to what sounds like a cold fact? To even doubt my former mentor for a moment feels terrible; it's a toxic cloud of poison suffocating me. What's the adage: if it sounds too good to be true, it is? This is the diametric opposite of what sounds good. It doesn't make it any less true. A question rises through the fog of heavy thought.

"Why the park?"

"Antoni believes..." he drags in a deep inhale. "He's overheard intel that Tatrialny will target the kids of every parliamentary member who denies support for legislation key to their operations."

Shock is a knife to my spine, seizing me with its power. I look away and out the window toward the moon, which hangs outside. I think of the sunny afternoon, the children running with glee, with freedom. I think of the home where I was abandoned, how my life would have turned out differently if I'd never left. For years, I have been safe, carving out a life for myself that did not resemble its beginnings on a stone-lined stoop. Something sharp dislodges itself in the center of me, unearthing from a long hibernation. Safety had sheltered me, made me soft. I had no use for softness now, not if I wanted to stop the people so set on destroying lives to make their profit.

My eyes return to Henry's with a slow-growing resolve. I wouldn't give in to fatalism. It feels as if everything that happens next hinges on how forcefully I'm willing to shove my heart back into my chest.

"Tell me what we need to do."

CHAPTER FOURTEEN

SOUTH OF FRANCE, PRESENT DAY

When he turns to face me, my heart is hammering against bone and flesh. In the light of the kitchen, Henry is staring down the barrel of my gun. Lowering my arm, the world is a sudden vacuum of sound and light. There is only him.

I rush toward him, and his arms wrap around me as we melt to the ground. It's not until he touches my cheeks that I realize I'm crying. My gasps tumble into sobs.

Here, finally: relief. His fingers intertwine with mine. Every atom wants to press closer, so close that maybe it will fill in the hollow space in my chest where I have been alone all these months. My tears release every ounce of grief I'd kept contained inside me, untouchable, necessitated by the need to survive for over six months without him.

All I see or feel is him. His heartbeat. A familiar woodsy scent of autumn. Henry's hand tucks between us as I cry. It is an ugly sound that escapes, making me sound like an animal in mourning. I do not care. With his arms wound tight around me, I'm rocked until I slowly find my breath. His fingers lift my chin as he pulls back to look at me. Leaning in gently, he seems afraid I might push him away. When our lips meet, I feel the invisible force of longing behind our kiss. Love, lacing us together with anguish.

He rests his forehead against mine, fingers lightly tracing the scar at my temple. The same way he used to after Warsaw. I grip his hand, twisting the gold band on his ring finger. My own is empty without the one he'd given me a year ago.

"Tu étais où pendant tout ce temps?" he whispers against my mouth.

Where have you been all my life?

CHAPTER FIFTEEN

LONDON, ENGLAND, ONE YEAR EARLIER

At half past ten, I'm making my way down the streets of London at night, so sleepy that it makes me wish I too were at my own flat, cozy in bed. I'd been at the pub earlier with my friend James, but as soon as I'd received a familiar message from an unlisted number, *20:45 — EC's,* I threw out hurried apologies to catch the London Underground. The message was sent to my burner phone, the number of which only Henry knew. As had happened previously, the message self-deleted after five seconds. Gone, as if it had never been there at all.

The SIM card, in addition to the phone itself, had been purchased with cash and could not be associated with me in any traceable way. Turning off my personal mobile so my whereabouts can't be tracked, the phone screen goes dark.

In the six weeks since returning to London from Warsaw, the mottled bruises on my arms have fully healed. I'd returned with more than only scars, but also an ever-present suspicion that has become almost impossible to shake off. Paranoia had a firm hand on my neck, frequently making me check over my shoulder. Terrible things could happen anywhere, at any moment.

Exiting the Tube, I turn down a well-lit street, empty of pedestrians or cars at the late hour. It's nearing the end of May, and the evening sky is less dreary than it'd been earlier that day. Once I pass a neat row of semi-detached homes, I squint to locate a very specific gap. When I spy a long row of square hedges, I check both directions before discreetly ducking between them. At a darkened backdoor stoop, I swallow my breathless exertion of trying to remain unseen. I check my watch: 20:45 on the dot. An unspooling anxiousness rises in my chest with what awaits me in tonight's conversation. Before I can raise my hand to knock, Emerson wordlessly opens the door and shuts it wordlessly behind me.

"Henry's already in the sitting room." It's the only greeting I receive before he turns on his heel in the opposite direction. The three of us have only met twice since Warsaw. There'd been updates on the investigation of the bomb, but without DNA or any fingerprints on the explosive device, the particles recovered are useless. Henry has already briefed Emerson, including the chilling reason why that park, and others, are being targeted by Tatrialny. According to Henry, Emerson's resistance to notify various governments is MI6's directive to control the narrative and contain what we know. Desperation claws at me to save everyone we can, but it's another wounding reminder that Emerson might actually be dangerous.

I follow Emerson's lead, each room dimly lighting the way toward the far end of the house. We walk past a flight of stairs, and I know Helen is likely upstairs. They were married long before he began his service in MI6, so I imagine Helen's aware of the discretion and privacy required with Emerson's role. I force myself to relax and be measured in my responses tonight, but anxiety is a steady companion. What if Emerson figures out what I know? That Henry and I are working together because of a conspiracy that Emerson is trying to feed information to—or worse, help—Tatrialny?

We enter the windowless sitting room, with lamps in each corner. I quickly wipe my sweaty palms on the back of my skirt. Henry looks up from whatever he's reading. Since that night in the hotel room in Warsaw, I know there are things I can and must withhold from Emerson and MI6 as a whole. It feels wrong. Even though Henry outlined how it would have to be once we returned to London, the falsity required feels more insurmountable by the minute. It's distressing to know the believability of my performance is equal to the stakes. I tamp my fear down and shove it into a small box inside myself. A lot of lives depend on this.

"You're late," Henry says, with a brief flicker of his eyes at me before returning to the papers in his hands. My eyes tighten at the remark. Fortunately, there's no false performance in my irritation with him. Just because we have to work together doesn't mean I've forgiven him for last fall.

I welcome the drink Emerson pours and take a seat. He indicates the reading material in Henry's hands and takes a seat in the chair next to him.

"Agent Clark and I were just discussing access to the device," Emerson tells me.

"Any progress on accessing the information on it yet?" I ask, even though I already know the answer. Since Warsaw, Henry has been trying to connect with his informant Antoni to get more information on the advanced technology. I look between them.

"Not as of yet," says Henry. He flips one last page before lowering it to the coffee table. "However, I have a contact who was willing to analyze the device. It is... far more fragile than we initially anticipated. There's a self-destruction component."

Memories flash at his choice of words: laughter in a park, the smell of burnt metal, a thunderous blast still rattling in my sternum after all these weeks.

"What kind of component are we talking about?" Asks Emerson, who glances at the shock of my expression and turns to Henry.

"There's a module in the software that, if accessed improperly, will detonate," explains Henry, his eyes briefly meeting mine. "The device seems to be made up of lithography technology, which means access isn't granted simply by connecting it to a computer."

"Like a lithograph?" I ask in confusion. "As in print-making, like on a metal plate?"

"A bit like that, except they inverted it. This lithography technology shrinks device dimensions while simultaneously minimizing algorithmic deficiencies. Whoever created this thing knew its elements could serve multiple purposes; it consumes little power, but it also points to the data being so securely encoded that the risk of damaging it is high. My source was able to get me the device, but not the key to unlocking it."

"So if access is possible, are we saying it's going to take... what—months to access the data? Half a year?" I ask, gripping the drink in my hand. I need to know the answer, but I already know I'm going to hate it.

"A few months at minimum, a year at the most," says Henry, who seems just as bothered about this as I am. "There's also something else I've learned, which is that this particular tech has a higher storage density. We could be talking about hundreds of thousands of pages of information. It's going to take a while to cull through everything. And that's *if* we can get in at all."

Emerson sits back, his elbow resting on the arm of his chair. I watch Emerson, who seems to be taking the information in stride. Meanwhile, my attempt at playing catch-up is like doing mental math that only leaves me feeling... mental.

"Then we'll have to get creative," I add in, unsolicited. "I'm no expert, but surely there's an alternative way to go about it, or a key that allows us a safe entry point to access—"

"—Given that the elements of the device are foreign to us, this is tricky technology," Henry emphasizes. "It comes with high risk if we get it wrong."

While I approve of Henry's ability to relay bad news without an overlong preamble, I'm resentful of another obstacle that feels insurmountable. For weeks, we've had it, and for weeks, we've been unable to access its information. Our greatest challenge has been finding out how this device works. Its oval shape is unlike anything either of us has ever seen before—nothing resembling what's circulating even in the black markets, Henry told me a few weeks ago. Knowing that we could easily destroy it and all its contents terrifies me. What's the point of any of this if we fuck it up?

"There have been hints and progress of this technology for years," says Emerson. "Clark is right. We will only get one chance at this, so it's vital we're careful, even if it costs us time."

I peer into my glass with a desperate kind of helplessness. Time isn't the only consequence...

"There are possibilities, however," adds Henry. "My informant is going to attempt to procure the key to access. And in the meantime, there might be a means of creating a key fob. The fob would generate an electronic signal that would allow us to remote in."

My head snaps up. "*Now* you tell us?" I ask icily. I want to kill him.

"I could foresee issues with traceability of a fob, as it's a highly regulated technology," Emerson comments, scratching at his chin. "Traceability is also at issue, given that Tatrialny is embedded in several industries. We need more information about how to access the data, and also what other technology might show our hand while trying to gain access."

"Exactly," Henry rises abruptly from his chair.

My eyes are lasers pointing at his back as he moves to refill his drink from the bar cart. When he turns, I glance away.

"Let's dig into this a bit more," adds Emerson. "See what you can find out until our next meeting, Clark. I think you should leave the device with me in the meantime."

My blood runs cold at his request. We'd anticipated this might happen. Despite the wager I'd made myself in support of Emerson's innocence, that if he didn't ask for the device, it meant Henry was wrong. My hands bite into my palms at the idea that Emerson might know that the information on it puts him at risk. It's a steel weight in the pit of my stomach.

"I've placed it in a secure location, sir," says Henry, who doesn't look at me. "When would you like me to bring it?"

"What if further analysis is needed?" I ask, as if I'm trying to be helpful and not purposefully direct Emerson's attention to me. "If a fob is an alternative with any merit, wouldn't it make more sense for Henry to retrieve it at the soonest possible moment?"

"MI6 resources are a possibility," says Emerson, his face schooling back into its thoughtful demeanor. "If we're calculating risks, we want to do this on this side of soon. Clark, why don't you bring it to me tomorrow, first thing?"

"Are we certain that utilizing MI6 technology for the device would be a closed loop?" I ask. "Don't we want to be careful to contain it to us three until we can get access through other methods?" I'm afraid I've gone too far, and I try not to swallow when Emerson's eyes narrow in my direction. *Be normal,* I tell myself. *Don't appear guilty.*

"It's a reasonable point," says Emerson finally. Fingers scratch at his brow, and he looks to Henry. "Keep it safe for now, and we'll revisit it in a few months if there's no success. Stay in contact with your informant and keep a close eye on any possible whispers of another attack."

Like a traitor, my lungs deflate with immense relief that somehow Henry and I have convinced him. Emerson turns his attention back to me.

"Amara, where are we at with the review of upcoming legislation for Hungary?"

"Yes, sir," I say, pulling out my laptop to refer to my notes. I begin to parse through the documentation I'd made. "Regarding the gaps of particular interest to us, we'll want to focus on..."

For the remainder of the meeting, I can feel Henry's watchful gaze, but I pretend he's not even in the room.

***

I'm only two blocks from my flat when I get a call on my disposable. With a glance over my shoulder, it's only me and the quiet roads of South Kensington.

"You could have fucking warned me," I answer.

"Hello to you, too, darling," says Henry. "Nearly home?"

"Cut the shit," I say scathingly. "Why didn't you tell me beforehand about the self-destruction module? That's a pretty crucial detail I should know before a meeting with Emerson."

"I only just found out," he tells me. "Not to mention, you're not a very good liar. Emerson can't doubt any of my work on the investigation with him, and he can't know you're in on this with me.

He needs to believe the truth of what we choose to share, but only when we deem it strategic. ”

I can’t deny the logic of his statement, but it, like so much else about him, is another thing that pisses me off. I don’t trust him, and I feel bitterly resentful of the idea that Emerson, my mentor and friend, has betrayed his country while I’m stuck trying to work in secret with Henry.

“You’re angry with me,” says Henry with a kind of regret in his voice.

“I’m only surprised you’ve made it this long in life without someone making an attempt on yours,” I say blithely.

He sighs through the phone. “All right—let's have it.”

“I felt foolish in that room,” I say. “I understand the approach needs to be delicate; however, we agreed in Warsaw that we had to keep open lines of communication in order to do this. Withholding the truth from me because you think I can’t handle it wildly undermines my involvement. You should have told me. How else can I actively participate in this case if you make choices without consulting me?”

Silence.

Then, “Okay—you’re right. I'm sorry.”

“Not to mention—” I stop. “You’re apologizing.”

“Don’t let it shock you too much.” A deep laugh rumbles through the phone.

“A shame,” I tell him as I walk through the door of my building and get onto the lift, “I had at least ten more minutes of haranguing in me."

"I should have trusted that you might know how to react and told you before the meeting. I agree with you."

"Tell me more about the key fob," I pivot back to the topic at hand as I arrive on my floor. "Is that a viable option?"

"Antoni still might be able to get the key programmed to it, so trying to create a fob specifically for it isn't ideal. Emerson was telling the truth; it's highly regulated security technology, and we don't know the scale of industries Tatrialny dips their hands into."

Walking into the door of my flat, I remove my shoes and toss my keys on the kitchen counter.

"Believe me when I say that my only goal is to avoid triggering the software that would cause the device to self-destruct," says Henry seriously. "Antoni is finding a way to at least get us access to partial data."

Can I really trust him over Emerson? I'd built years of communication and rapport with him. Now I'm supposed to trust the man I'd seen kiss another woman?

"Partial data isn't nothing, but it might prevent us from seeing the whole picture," I say. The whole picture being that, deep down, I really don't want Emerson's involvement with Tatrialny to be true.

"I'm working on it," he tells me. "To find out who Emerson's protecting, we need every bit of intel possible. I'll see if I can get more information from Antoni."

My stomach grumbles, and I peek into my pantry and fridge. Both have nearly empty shelves.

"I'll find a way to research as well," I say, thinking of the library.

"Let me know if you have any success. Aside from the tech expert I'm utilizing, you will be the first to know what I find. Is that a packet of biscuits I hear?"

I freeze, a thin cracker halfway to my mouth.

"Yes, I'm *starving*. I had to run out of a pub to be at Emerson's on time."

Moving toward the large floor-to-ceiling windows, I watch London's roving lights ten floors below. Even at night, when the city is in slumber, its midnight view is a thrill.

"What else is for dinner?" he asks.

"Smoked gouda," I tell him between another bite. "And goat cheese bits."

"Not a fan of either," he says. "I'm more of a cottage cheese gentleman."

I stop mid-chew. "Cottage cheese of *all* the cheeses?"

"It's good for you."

"How am I supposed to trust anything you say now?"

His voice lowers conspiratorially. "You can act indifferent all you want, but I know a secret no one else does."

"Oh?"

"I know you're secretly fond of me."

A kick drum resounds in my chest, and my face grows warm.

"If I am," I say impartially, "It's only in the way one is fond of a street dog. It's hard not to feel bad for the poor thing."

Henry chuckles. "I'm sure that's it."

Now properly satisfied, I've grown tired. Setting the cheese and crackers down, I flop with my back onto the sofa. "It's late," I say.

"It is," he says. "I've a meeting at headquarters tomorrow before leaving for Jordan."

"All right."

"It'll only be a week," he says casually. "Then I'll be back."

"Why are you telling me?" I say with a shrug, even though he can't see it. "I didn't ask to know."

"That's why I'm telling you. So you don't have to."

I give a noncommittal hum.

"See you tomorrow, Amara," he says, then hangs up without waiting for me to say it back.

Staring at the screen for a long moment after the call ends, I rest the phone in the soft, fleshy middle between my ribcage. I think of a sensual evening last fall that still haunts me like a ghost, and reminds me that Henry's ability to keep secrets is the first thing I learned about him. I resent its usefulness now. I resent, too, acknowledging how necessary it is, in his job, to keep secrets to keep people safe. I close my eyes. Maybe I would loathe him less if he could stop keeping secrets from *me*.

Chapter Sixteen

Standing against the countertop, I wait, bleary-eyed, for coffee to finish brewing. The sixth floor of Vauxhall Cross is quiet so far this morning. After the late-night meeting and subsequent conversation with Henry, fatigue hangs heavy on both eyelids. I'd fallen asleep on the sofa, a starless night out my windows. Waking up to the glaring dawn of morning with a sudden panic that I'd overslept had been a rude awakening.

"Had a good time for yourself last night, eh?" Says a voice. I look up to see one of the agents in headquarters, Tobias, walk into the common room. His lip curls with amusement as he turns on the electric kettle.

Covering my yawn with the back of my hand, I give a vague sort of nod. No extra effort needed to convince him, since he's mostly paying attention to his phone. Excellent, maybe I can leave before he notices—

He raises his head as if on cue. "How goes it today?" His voice is smooth, well-practiced in the art of, I assume, talking to people even when they're trying to get away. "Are you usually here this early?"

"Not usually," I say as I reach into the refrigerator. "How are you?"

He grabs a clean mug from the cupboard. "Do you know, I'm quite good. Oh, could you be a darling and grab the milk for me?"

Cringing inwardly, I straighten, thrusting the carton into his hands. With steam rising from my own mug, I begin casually shuffling toward the double doors of the common room.

"Well, I'll leave you to it then—"

He is either too obtuse to notice or is unfamiliar with social cues, because now he's shaking out a tin for the last tea bag while he's chattering on about one thing or another: a theater he's been to recently, a dinner spot not worth the three-digit price tag. Yet, to even politely listen to him, I'm faced with the fact that he's really quite tall. Tall enough that it requires me to angle my line of sight higher than usual, straining my tired eyes in the direction of the office's fluorescent lights. I run out of patience and energy as he splashes milk into his tea.

"My condolences for your inadequate dinner selection," I say with the thinnest veil of sincerity to get me out of the interaction. "I've got emails and such, so I'll be off—"

He takes a step back, interrupting my path to the door.

"I heard a few are heading to a pub later. Think you'll go?"

"I try not to commit to anything before noon," I say, emphasizing the point with my coffee.

He chuckles in response. "You should join, it'll be a good time—"

"Morning. How're we getting on today?"

With a glance over Tobias's shoulder, Henry walks toward us. Despite knowing I would see him, now that he's here in the flesh, I feel a flush of surprise. He arrives like a shadow, with a quality that charges the air in the room. I pretend not to notice.

"Mind?" Henry reaches around Tobias for a mug and pours himself a coffee.

Leaning against the counter where I'd been standing earlier, his eyes fix on Tobias. He hasn't sent an acknowledging glance my way, which is for the best, since we're not friends. I mean, we're hardly friendly anyway, but for the sake of the operation, public perception is more important than the truth.

"Can I help you with something, mate?" Tobias asks at his stare.

"Don't mind me, *mate*," says Henry, though he disarms his tone with a layer of intimidation and a smile that flashes white teeth. Like a wolf.

Suddenly, my morning becomes unexpectedly pleasant and entertaining. Tobias is about to give some kind of retort when a few other staff walk in.

"Amara, did you make coffee already?" Madeline, a fellow solicitor on my team, chirps energetically, her blonde hair swishing at her shoulders. "You're an angel."

I give Madeline a smile. Welcoming the distraction as a good moment to duck out, I leave without even a final, fleeting glance at Henry or Tobias before heading to my office and shutting the door. My closed door is as close to an official do-not-disturb notice as it gets. Opening the blinds to a window behind my desk, the gray, mercurial sky is a handprint against the tempered glass. After logging onto the server, much of the day is spent on emails and diplomatic documents from foreign embassies. In the final hour before I typically wrap up at the office, a buzzing notification interrupts my focus. There's nothing on the screen.

Ah, right. I swivel in my chair and pull out the disposable phone from inside my desk drawer, where I'd placed it earlier. I read a message from a random number.

Meet me tomorrow evening. 10 o'clock. Greenwich.

The demanding undertone grates on my nerves. I don't hesitate to send a reply.

Are you trying to get stabbed? You might as well have suggested Croydon.

Don't worry. If anyone tries to stab me, I'll make sure you have the first go.

I don't budge. *Somewhere else.*

After two minutes with no reply, I wonder if he'll simply ignore me. While I understand the necessity for discretion, I loathe that it equals limited options for places to meet. Despite my irritation with him, I know I could never blow off a meeting to discuss the mission. His silence would force me to meet him in a dodgy part of London, but I wouldn't have to like it.

Just then, another message. *Taro Bowl. The West End.*

With a concise search on an open-source network to scramble my location, I scroll through a few photos and reviews of the restaurant. A Chinese spot to the north. Perhaps one of the more touristy parts of London, but given the hour, it would be considerably less crowded. For any foot traffic, it means no one will look twice at me, and it would be easier to avoid being distinctly seen in any CCTV footage later, if it came to that. My fingers hover on the phone. The covert investigation Henry and I are working on occupies a lot of my headspace, but does he think I have nothing better to do than meet in some dingy place on a Saturday evening?

It is true, of course, though I hate to think he knows it.

A familiar sensation of shame pricks at my neck. I get along with colleagues fine, sometimes even go for a drink at a pub here and there. James is one of the few people I can count as a real friend. Otherwise, they're few and far between. For much of my time, I am by myself. No husband. No children. No pets. My life does not conform to the regular standard of most people I know. Even being adopted did not put an end to the melancholy layer of how I experience the world. I didn't *choose* to be left with strangers and given up in Warsaw. How I came into the world—alone, in the dead of winter—meant any wish I had to know my parents was like walking around with a blindfold. I was not imaginative enough to conjure details of who my parents are.

There's a certain rationality to abandonment; it strips away all romantic notions that hardship was going to make me exceptional. That any success I gained in life was a modern-day story of resilience, meant to shine against the lonely smudge of foster care. Sometimes bad things just happen. And they happened to me. Reality comes in the shape of emotion that lodges itself in my throat at the idea that my life could have turned out any differently. No matter that being in social settings makes me feel like an alien cosplaying as a person. No matter that I am always somewhere outside the happy chatter, existing on the periphery of belonging that everyone else feels is assumed.

I type out a response.

I'll be at Taro Bowl. I hope the food is better than the pun.

Without waiting for a reply, I place the phone back in the drawer behind some files. A knock sounds at my office door.

"Come in." I turn to my computer screen as if I'd been working. I look up to see Madeline. "Here to go over next week's meeting agenda?"

With a laugh and a shake of her head, she says, "Hell no." She leans a hand on the doorknob. "I wanted to invite you out. A few of us are heading to the pub."

"I heard the rumor this morning from Tobias," I tell her.

"Don't mind him. He grew up posh, so he evokes a natural irritation," says Madeline with a wink before straightening. "Want to join, anyway? There are a few others going. Why don't we get some fresh air on a Friday night?"

"I don't know," I say. I had been hoping to go home, especially after last night's late night. "Going far?"

"Near Kennington Park," she replies, waving her hand over her shoulder. "Too many toddlers whining about crossing the Thames."

A polite decline is on the tip of my tongue. Logically, there's an advantage to going, since we still need to determine whether

Emerson is protecting someone in MI6. If I'm honest, it's more than that, though. I think of Henry's message and an evening alone in my flat, and I'm overcome by the urge not to sit in the quiet.

"Sure," I say.

If she's surprised by me accepting the invitation, she doesn't show it. She grins, releasing her hand from the doorknob. "Excellent. Why don't we walk there together?"

"Sure," I say. "Let me grab my things, and I'll meet you at the elevators?"

She turns with a wave of agreement. I save my work and log out of the server. Making sure no one is outside my door, I quickly hide the disposable phone in an inner pocket of my bag, feeling duplicitous, as if not only does my loneliness wear a mask, but now so does the rest of my life, too.

Chapter Seventeen

When we arrive, the pub in Lambeth is noisy, a mix of families and glasses clinking against plates. A row of taps is being tended, while TVs on two walls are showing a football game. Dark wooden benches flank two long tables, and separate tables with booths are farther back.

"A few of us are already here," says Madeline, pointing toward a booth.

"Know what you'd like?" I ask her, gesturing to the bar. "I'll grab us drinks."

"I'll start off easy with a cider. I'll get the next round!" she says with a smile before heading to the table.

As I near the counter, an untidy queue is beginning to form. People jostle past each other toward the bar as others carry off with their beers. I'll never get used to London, all the pressing of bodies in what little space exists. By the time I'm pushing through the crowd with two ciders in hand, the pub has become considerably busier. I notice Madeline waving at me to make sure I see where they're sitting. The mark of the weekend has brought the city through the door, and I squeeze in around chairs toward the booth.

A few others from headquarters have joined while I've been ordering drinks, including Tobias. He's speaking to the table, and a wide smile cracks across his face, almost making him look like a completely different person. At the table, I recognize Tom, Emerson's chief of staff, and Nora, a technologist. I take a seat between Nora and Madeline and hand her the other cider.

"—complete bollocks, that. It should at least be a *good* one," Tobias says, which lands him some guffaws around the table.

"What's bollocks?" I inquire curiously.

Tobias is about to say, but Tom beats him to it with a grin. "In order to tell the story, Amara, I'll need to take you back to three years ago, when a poorly made shooter game caused such an uproar it forced the company to release a *new* game for fear of angering fans to the point of revolution—"

"Ignore Tom and his conversational side streets," says Nora with a laugh. "I was saying there was a short-lived concern about recent web traffic a few weeks ago. Our system can differentiate games from real events, obviously," she adds, "but there was a cluster of activity relating to some aggressive keywords that our system was picking up. There are always several things to monitor with interest, but someone on the team forgot to do a background check on local events in Birmingham."

"What was happening in Birmingham?" I ask.

Nora's light eyes crinkle with humor. "A meeting of high-level nerds."

"You mean a gaming convention," corrects Tom.

"As the resident nerd among us, those terms are mutually exclusive," says Nora, throwing back her head with a laugh.

"Are we permitted to know how an event like that impacts what you do?" Madeline tilts her head to look around me at Nora. "I'm so curious."

"Well, when there's a concentrated population in an area, there's an increase in devices. There's always monitoring of certain hubs, though there are a lot of variables at play, depending on current events or incidents," explains Nora.

"Seems like a rookie mistake to confuse a gaming convention for a real security concern, no?" Asks Tobias as he leans forward on his elbows with an interested expression. "Aren't there things set in place to prevent false alarms?"

She shrugs, probably guessing that scenarios like this one would affect his work in the field elsewhere.

"A minor one. Though it did lead to an interesting observation about web traffic out of Eastern Europe. So it actually worked out."

Immediately, her words are a magnet to my attention. I take a sip of my drink and casually look around as if I'm more interested in the game playing on the TV than Nora's response.

"Well, come on then, don't leave us hanging," teases Madeline over the din of the pub. "Let me guess—*another* gaming convention?"

"Not bloody work talk," says Tobias, and Tom, sitting beside him, also groans.

"Hmm." I turn to Nora in time to see a contemplative look sweep across her face as it melts into a frown. "Well—without divulging specifics, I suppose perhaps I can say one thing. There was some activity to the east of us a few weeks ago, but it passed. We thought it might be related to an explosion in Poland, but local intelligence is telling us it's not related, and the investigation was closed after they found the suspect dead. There was residue of the bomb on his hands. It's all public, though; a local newspaper even published his picture."

My heart beats rapidly. They found someone? The investigation is closed? I bookmark it to mention to Henry later.

"Can you say what they were investigating—?" Madeline starts, then stops herself, waving her hand dismissively in the air. "Don't answer that. Sorry—habit as a solicitor to ask questions."

"I think I heard quite a few people were killed," says Tom with a slightly gloomy expression.

I feel a heat on my neck warming me like a fire lights my clothes. The air is nearly stifling among the noise and the laughter of strangers around us. Focusing on my breath, I keep my eyes glued to the bottom of my glass. I want to drink it all until it's completely empty, until the smell of melted metal and a terrifying silence no longer haunts me. I realize I've not been paying attention to the conversation.

"The one in Poland, right?" Tobias asks grimly. "It's hard to keep track of all the shitty things going on lately."

"Yeah, in Warsaw," says Nora. "Very sad, actually. Was likely politically motivated and tied to a local election, though it was near a school."

Our table turns to an uncomfortable silence. *Breathe,* I tell myself. *Nothing bad can happen here. You're safe, you're fine.*

"Now that we're all properly cheered up by this topic of conversation, who wants another round?" Tobias stands from his chair and points at each of us. His own drink is gone, a small puddle of condensation beneath the glass.

Next to me, Madeline's own drink is gone. "Cider, for me, please, but I was supposed to get the next round."

"On me." Tobias waves her off.

"I'll take a porter if you're buying," says Tom with a quick grin.

"Same for me, cider," I say as I point to Madeline's glass.

"None for me, thanks," Nora declines with a shake of her head.

Tobias nods and heads off to order drinks for the table. Madeline turns to Nora and me. "Do you know if you're going to the agency gala next month?"

"I might do, yeah," Nora says with a glance at her phone. "Shit. I need to be off, I have an early morning." She rises to stand.

"Work tomorrow?" I ask.

"Worse," she says, finishing the last bit of her drink. "I'm going to brunch with my mother-in-law."

Nora rises from her seat and departs with a friendly goodbye to us three, and waves to Tobias at the bar on her way out the door. When he returns, he sets the drinks in the center of the table and slides into Nora's vacated seat. Tom and Madeline are animatedly watching the football game.

"Thank you," I say politely, reaching for a glass of cider.

"I believe this is the longest amount of time I've seen you outside of headquarters," comments Tobias as he takes a sip of his drink. "Are you usually averse to socializing with colleagues?"

I halt mid-sip. "Just because you haven't seen me, doesn't mean I don't socialize."

Right as cheers and shouts break out behind us, his phone screen lights up from a call. A glance at the TV tells me that Chelsea scored. He slides it off the table and places it in his back pocket.

"You are a bit quiet, though," Tobias comments thoughtfully. "It reminds me a little of my sister. Well, half-sister."

"Are you two close?" The fact that he has a sister surprises me. He's always struck me as an only child.

"Not particularly." He swills the liquid in his glass before taking a sip. "We didn't grow up together. Same father, different mother. Not terribly close with my father either."

When he raises his gaze to mine, I realize his eyes look... sad. Among the discordant sounds of the game and chatter from the bar, I kind of feel sorry for him. It makes me regret my earlier curtness. I would know better than most that trying to connect with people can feel messy sometimes, especially when family life is a bit unconventional or distant.

"What about friends?" I ask with interest. "Maybe from uni?"

"Sure, a few," he says with a nonchalant shrug. "It's hard to keep friends, though, when you move around a lot. Changing schools didn't help."

"I get that," I say truthfully. "I grew up in Poland, then was adopted by an American family when I was six."

He studies me. "Do you speak any Polish?"

"Well, sure, but I have the accent of an American," I say with a laugh, and he laughs with me. The conversation is pleasant, far easier than any of our previous interactions. "I did study the language in undergrad, but I neither wanted to teach nor work as a translator. When I received a full scholarship for law school, I decided to pursue a degree in international law. Seemed far more interesting to me."

"A scholarship of that size—is that rare?" he asks with surprise.

"I don't know really," I say as I think about it. "Perhaps? It was unusual more so because I didn't apply for it. The scholarship sort of..." I gesture around me vaguely, "...fell into my lap. The school said there was a large sum donation from a foundation."

My phone rings on the table. I check who's calling, and it's an unfamiliar number with a Polish country code. My heart thuds in my chest.

"It's good," Tobias is saying. Something about his tone is forced, and I wonder if he's thinking of his own family. "It all worked out well for you."

"Sorry—I need to take this." I point to my phone and rise. Madeline notices and smiles at me before returning to argue about the game with Tom. I duck out of the pub before the call can go to voicemail.

"Hello?"

"Is this Amara?" A woman asks with a thick accent. A group of kids passes just then, laughing loudly on the sidewalk.

"This is." I walk the other direction and press the phone closer to my ear. There's no response for a long moment, and I'm afraid the call has dropped until I check the screen. We're still connected. "Can you hear me?"

"Yes, yes," says the woman. "My name is Irena. I received your... ah, information from *Dom Dziecka*. I was told you are seeking information about the night you came to the home?"

A breath catches sharply in my lungs. While I hadn't forgotten about my visit to the orphanage in Warsaw, some part of me had given up hope. My mind races to catch up to the rest of what she's saying.

I switch to Polish. "Did you—did you work there when I was there?" My voice sounds far stronger than I feel.

"I did, yes." A pause. "I was the one who took you in."

My words stumble out. "I've been waiting a long time to speak with you. Can you tell me anything about that night? Anything at all that you remember?"

"I will do my best. It was a long time ago," she says, her voice gentle through the phone. "I can say that your mother was very young. It was late, and she knocked many times before I answered the door. You were crying. You were so new, so young. She had likely given birth to you only hours before."

I picture it: a young mother, a baby wrapped in a blanket, in the night.

"Did she say what her name was?"

"She did not," the woman says, and I feel a sagging disappointment.

"Did she say why she couldn't keep me?" My fingers grip the phone. I have waited for so long that it seems impossible that the moment has finally come. A long silence follows, and I worry the call has dropped. "Irena?"

She finally speaks. "You must understand—I have never told anyone this before." I detect an unpleasant emotion in her words. Like a voice caught between a shout and a whisper.

"Is there something wrong?"

"I have never told this to anyone because the night after your mother left you with me, she was found dead," she says. "That is how I found out her name."

The news is like walking into a brick wall that comes out of nowhere. "What—she—" I say, trying to process what she's saying. "How did you find out she died?"

"It was in the papers," Irena says carefully. "There was a suspicious car accident not far from the home. I recognized her picture immediately. That is how I found out your mother's name was Valeria Grala, and I have never forgotten it."

My entire life has been spent wondering, imagining, inventing who my mother was. As a child, I would write names on sheets of paper, practicing cursive letters across the alphabet. Every bookstore I visited meant combing through the international section, a finger on an author's name across the spine, wondering if one day I might guess correctly. Someone who was too famous for a child, maybe an actress too beloved to devote time to a crying baby. Never once had I guessed Valeria. Never once did I think she had died. I had lacked the imagination for the scope of my grief.

There's something about the way she's telling me about my mother's death that strikes me as strange. "Why suspicious?"

"When the paper announced the accident, I suddenly understood the fear in her eyes," says Irena.

"She was afraid for herself?"

"No," she says, her voice becoming stronger, louder in my ear than all the traffic of London. "When I saw her that night, I believed she was afraid for her life. After I saw the news of her death, I realized she was afraid for yours."

CHAPTER EIGHTEEN

Less than 24 hours later, I am crossing Trafalgar Square in the rain, the evening as soggy as my mood. My umbrella shields me from CCTV cameras. The wet sidewalks spill into cracks and gutters, and my eyes dart both ways before crossing the road. Taking a shortcut through an alley, I leave behind the tourist crowds and come upon Taro Bowl. I shake out the umbrella and duck inside.

The restaurant is fairly empty, save for a few patrons here and there in its worn, faded booths. The front is empty of any staff. A pile of plastic menus lies next to a half-torn receipt. Walls curve up toward the ceiling, which is covered in glowing paper lanterns. The globes emit a crimson shade, casting eerie shadows above my head. I spot Henry, who is partially obscured with his back to the door, though truthfully, I easily recognize him, probably because of how often I've thrown curses at the back of his head. Striding over to where he's sitting at a booth in the far corner, I take a seat opposite him. I'm ready to argue, and most importantly, ready to eat.

"Did you check to see if anyone was following you?" he asks by way of greeting.

Arguing first, it is, then.

"Well, I thought it would be better if I posted my location on social media." I smile sweetly. My saccharine tone draws an arching brow from him, though he doesn't look up from the stained menu in his hands.

"If this is my last meal, then perhaps I'll get both bao buns and beef shumai." He briefly glances at my handbag. "And did you—"

"—turn my phone off to prevent tracking from cell towers?" I ask, tugging the menu out of his hands to give it a look over. "Give me some fucking credit, Henry."

Reaching across the table, he grabs an order card from a stack against the wall. After marking a few boxes, he spins it toward me. Marking a few as well, I insert the order card into a narrow metal slot built into the table. A small light blinks red until a waiter soundlessly shuffles over and takes the card without looking at us. They trod off, out of sight.

"Not even water, yeah?"

"Probably better we didn't."

"The water's not safe, but you're suggesting the *food* is fine?"

He eyes me. I eye him back.

Setting the menu aside, I lean against the vinyl padding.

"I have news. Last night I learned that the local inquiry into the bomb in Warsaw has been closed."

This appears to be news to him. "For what reason?"

My eyes rise upward as I try to remember Nora's phrasing. "...was likely politically motivated and tied to the local election. A suspect was confirmed dead near the scene with, allegedly, residue on their fingers that matches residue from the bomb."

"A bloody, fucking lie."

I hesitate. "You don't think—"

"—that the person found dead is our man?" He shakes his head with a sigh. "No, I don't."

"Incredibly convenient story, given what we know," I say. Some of my earlier ire deflates in my chest. Only now, I'm a different kind of angry. How could Emerson ever agree to help people who wanted to kill, maim, and harm? What the hell does he get out of it? "If the case is closed because the lone suspect is dead, that means the person actually responsible is still out there. We are running out of time."

"We are doing everything we can, as fast as we can." He keeps his voice low. "But it's important we do this very carefully. Not only because of Emerson, but also because of the risk of setting it off."

"Tell me more," I say, then point a finger at his chest. "This time, *don't* withhold."

He folds his hands into his lap. "I have a contact who was able to confirm an address."

"Antoni gave you an address for someone inside Tatrialny?" I ask.

He shakes his head. "Another contact. Someone in MI5."

"Is their name James?" I ask, knowing the answer is no, but my competitive streak can't let his comment stand.

"James works for MI5?" He looks at me over the table. "You never said."

I shrug. "There's a lot about me you don't know."

"So you keep telling me."

"You were saying," I say between bites. "An address?"

His eyes are intensely dark as they watch me. "Not for someone in Tatrialny. For a parliamentary leader who is *possibly* associated with someone inside the syndicate," he corrects. "Antoni has been passing as much intel my way that he can without jeopardizing himself."

"That means they could be anywhere," I say, panic slipping through. "Any country."

Right then, the waiter rolls over a cart, its surface covered in plateware. Steam rises through bamboo steamers. With an unceremonious *thud*, our food arrives with a heavy flourish. Green chives and soy sauce slosh against the sides of a ceramic serving dish like water against the hull of a ship. A few drops color the white cloth in an instant, their dark shape blooming unevenly. Once again, we're given privacy.

"I revise my earlier remark—" I start. "It's not thoughtlessness; they simply don't *care*."

"I know," he says between chews. "It's great."

"Any word yet?" I ask, changing the subject.

"Yes," he says, pointing his chopsticks at me. "But you must promise me something."

My hand brushes aside the utensil. "No."

"You haven't even heard yet."

"Nothing good will come out of promises to you."

He cocks his head. "Did something happen?"

"What?" I straighten. "No."

"You're more hostile than usual," he says, watching me.

"That is a mischaracterization," I tell him dispassionately. "I'm *always* this hostile to you."

"It isn't a criticism," says Henry rakishly, leaning toward me across the table with a wink. "I'm always in the mood for a row, darling. I just like a little warning first."

My eyes bore into his. No matter how I feel, there's no need to be fast and loose with my temper right now. We have more important matters to discuss. My fingers dig into my knees beneath the table as I force myself to relax.

"I promise, mostly. Now, what is it?"

"Don't overreact," he says, his eyes on mine. "I learned I'll have access to the data within the next few months. Perhaps sooner. And I know how to do it without triggering the detonation."

My chopsticks drop onto a dish, splashing more liquid onto the table.

"Amara."

"You found a way?"

"I did. Fobs with this technology *are* highly regulated and easy to trace," says Henry. I see the slow, gloating gleam in his eyes. "Except, when you know someone who works where the manufacturers build them."

"Where?"

"Japan."

"So you're saying this could really happen," I ask with more hope than I've had since Warsaw. "How do we make sure it will work?"

"There will be a test fob built at the manufacturer. My source and I will test a signal device that is nearly exact. The parts will be the same from the black market, to ensure our coding will work."

The reality of what is possible hits me. "And when you conduct a test, we'll be able to access the device, and..."

"Identify members of Tatrialny, as well as bills and governments to put our attention toward. It is our greatest countermeasure against them. It might hold any blackmail material they could have on Emerson," he says heatedly. "We have a chance to put a lot of dangerous people away."

While he eats, my mind drifts. Each time Emerson's name comes up, it is sandpaper on my skin. I realize he has betrayed his own country; it shocks me to face it, almost as if it were the first time all over again. Thoughts spin in circles like an ouroboros eating itself. It is staggering, and the fallout is immense. Emerson's involvement not only strips my ability to trust people but also destroys my trust in myself. I should have seen it, right? Something wayward, a deceiving quality where you know you're in the room with a predator. Never have I felt that from Emerson. Only warmth, as my former mentor, combined with the sharp intellect of someone who is the director of MI6.

"Penny for your thoughts," interrupts Henry.

My eyes shoot to his. The last person I'm going to speak with about anything is him. I hope the expression on my face conveys as much, so it can save me the trouble of explanation. It must, because he shrugs unbothered, finishing the last bite of a bao bun.

"Are you going to the gala in a few weeks?" he says.

"Not you, too," I groan.

"Well, I'll be there."

"Of course you will," I say, stealing the last shumai. "It's an opportunity for you to preen in every reflective surface you can find."

"It also happens to be a great *opportunity* to interact with unfamiliar staff in the agency," he says. "I think you should go too."

He has a point about that, and it wouldn't hurt to show my face a little bit more. Sitting across from me with a light and relaxed expression, I think of how Henry doesn't look like an agent at all. A question that has been tugging at me since we first met finally spills out.

"How did you get recruited?"

"...into this conversation?"

"Into the service," I say with an eye roll. "Obviously."

"It was in uni, actually. I was in my third year, studying finance—why are you laughing?" Dark hair falls over his forehead as he shifts in the booth, giving me a crooked smile.

I stifle my laugh and flourish a hand. Given his choice of suits, I can see it.

"Carry on."

Giving me a skeptical eye, he continues. "It's more sensical as an SIS officer if your background matches the story you're selling. It legitimizes an alias. Enemies always go digging to confirm if someone is who they say they are. What about you?"

"Mine is easier to guess," I say. "I was at Oxford studying law. Technically, I was on track to teach. Emerson approached me during my final year. He said there's been a private recommendation for me." I frown, remembering. "I'd forgotten about that, actually."

"Did you consider turning it down?"

"I didn't. I don't have family, so there was nothing taking me back to America. It seemed vital to devote myself to a career that was doing something important." I leave out the fact that it was Emerson who recruited me. I don't mention to Henry that it felt, for the first time in my life, as if something truly meaningful was happening to me. It was a drug. There was finally a purpose for me, and I was determined to fulfill it.

"Any news on that front?"

"About family?" My head tilts with confusion until I realize what he means. "What about it?"

"You can talk to me, you know. You don't have to be lonely." He swears under his breath at my tense expression. "Not what I meant. I'm saying you're not alone. I know what it's like to isolate yourself from others to survive."

"Don't talk about me as if I'm not sitting *right here*. I don't need the lecture. You really don't even know me."

"More than you think I do," he says softly. "It's not nothing. For what it's worth, you don't hide your feelings very well."

"What does that matter?"

"It matters because if you want to think like an agent, you have to behave like one. I'm not saying emotions don't have their place, but we have to be careful, Amara. Stupid things, *dangerous* things, happen when we're reckless."

At that, the slow burn of my earlier anger blazes back. "I think we're done here. In fact, I'd say we've been well and done for a year now." I stand abruptly without waiting for a reply.

Storming toward the door, it's the muted sound of his footsteps I hear first before his hand grips my arm. My elbow makes contact with a vase when I whirl on him. Henry catches it before it knocks into the ground. Taking one step toward me, his hand is still on my arm. I can see the white of his eyes boring into mine with an intensity like a needle tip gliding up my spine without breaking skin. His warm eyes focus on mine. It makes me even angrier to see the kindness there. It twists shame and regret in my chest. I shake him off, then turn without looking back.

I'm halfway down the alley when I realize I'd left my umbrella in the booth. Droplets fall into my eyes. Doesn't matter anyway; he can burn it for all I care. I keep walking. Water sloshes over my leather flats, soaking them as much as the rain drenches the city.

How fucking dare he? Why on earth would I want to discuss my family—or lack thereof—with him? Henry, who could barely be trusted? Henry, who lied and then went off to kiss another woman on the goddamn Tower Bridge?

I'm so upset that I don't realize there are splashes of footsteps behind me until they're at my back. With a roll of my eyes, I say as I turn, "I swear if you put another tracker in my phone—"

It's not Henry. The man before me is half a head taller, and he's wearing a mask. I keep my eyes on him and back away slowly.

"I wouldn't if I were you."

The man gives a low laugh, and the sound of it curls under the skin of my ears like fingers yanking for my attention. He takes a step forward, hands at his back as if he's simply taking a stroll. In the rain, streets are empty. Street lamps are beginning to turn. The sun wanes, disappearing out of sight. It's only me and him. He brings his arms forward. That's when I see a flash of a knife.

Could I run without falling? Rain splashes onto my lashes, and I blink them away. Would he catch me before I even took a step? The sidewalk is slick beneath my shoes. The moment my eyes dart to each side, he gives me a heavy *tsk*.

"Ah, ah," the man says, waving an index finger at me. "Let's not be naughty."

"Go fuck yourself." If this is it and I'm going to die, I won't do it by handing myself over on a platter.

"Excellent," the man says as he nears. Observing the way my feet move farther back, he says with a grin, "I always love a good chase."

Chapter Nineteen

Air lodges inside my lungs as if it were a fist. My hands grip the handbag strap across my chest. Rain spills from the darkening sky in an ominous foretelling. As the last of the day loses its light, his irises grow ominous and deliberate. My eyes dart around us, but there's no one else.

For a long time, I used to believe my parents might one day get sick of me, undo the adoption, and send me back to the home in Warsaw. I told myself I had to accept that surviving in this life meant expecting the worst. To always be ready for a fight, because if I relaxed, then I wouldn't be prepared to make it when something really bad happened.

The stranger is bulky, with a thick neck that meets hunching, massive shoulders. His unwavering attention tells me I am prey. I stand now before him and fear roils in my belly, like the aftertaste of bad whiskey. I had let myself become soft, and it is probably going to kill me. No matter where I've been, death has followed me, and I cannot evade its malevolent grasp.

Then: Another form, familiar in the shadows, appears.

I have never been so relieved to see Henry.

His hand quickly jabs at the man's throat, instant and injuring. It catches the man by surprise with a jolt. The man wheezes, gripping his neck with one hand as he whirls on Henry. The man's flailing breaths escape his lips as he punches his fist in Henry's direction, but his hand only meets the air that his lungs are gasping for. Henry is a blade of exactness, while the other man thrashes around with sheer force and a clear lack of precision. The sharp edge of his knife nearly meets Henry's ribcage. Henry lurches out of reach in time.

Henry once told me that agents in the service seldom carry a weapon, especially not a gun. For their operations and cover, an agent couldn't have something hidden in a pocket or a shoe, as it would be impossible to explain. Being found with one could have deadly consequences. With a sharp inhale, I know at this very moment that Henry has nothing but himself.

As the man's other hand loosens on his neck, he recovers quickly. He makes for another swipe, the large arc of his weapon tearing into the fabric of night between them. The usual aplomb that has always irritated me about Henry is useful now. His elbow jabs in the man's ribcage, followed by a slam of his foot flat against the back of the man's knee. But this stranger is difficult to disable. It's clear: it's easier to win in a fight if you have no qualms or morals. Henry's evasive moves are impressively agile, but it's hard to fight gravity and size. At the fourth attempt to evade, the tip of the man's blade makes a downward slice across Henry's arm. Instantly, it draws blood. With a hiss, Henry twists, placing himself out of reach again. It creates just enough distraction for the stranger to turn and run. He's fast, even with the rain, and is rapidly out of sight.

"Are you okay?" I gasp out. His arm is clearly bleeding now, dripping out onto the sidewalk. His hand uselessly presses against the wound.

Henry's eyes scan behind and around me. "We need to get out of here. Your flat is around the corner, right?"

The last time he'd been there with me was a painful poke of memory. But I know I have some bandages and wound care in a closet. I give a jolting nod, then shift in the direction of home. I've taken only a few steps when I realize he's not walking with me.

"What are you doing?" I ask as he holds a hand against his bleeding arm.

"There are cameras everywhere in London," he says just loud enough for me to hear. "I'll go around separately and meet you inside."

I think quickly. "The west entrance of the garage goes below my building. The code is 2480. There's a lift down there. If you take it to the 9th floor, there's a stair that's vacant and under construction. You can take it one floor up to mine."

He leaves, and I make the final stretch to my flat by myself. I turn on lamps in the bedroom and the entryway. In the bathroom, my eyes are red-rimmed. I splash cool water on my face, but it doesn't shake me out of my trembling. At a brief, single knock, a moment later, I'm ushering Henry in. Pushing him to sit on the sofa, I grab two hand towels, antibiotics, and rubbing alcohol. The sight of the blood again makes me queasy.

"You don't have to—" he starts to say, but my hands shove the materials into his before he can finish.

"Oh, I won't, trust me."

He sets a few of the items down on the coffee table. His movements are precise, elegant. The rubbing alcohol spills neatly onto one of the cloths. Cleaning his wound, he hardly reacts to the pain. Setting it on the surface of the table, Henry pulls on the other cloth and, letting out a tight sigh, presses the clean fabric against his arm. I don't know what to do with my hands as I watch. He glances at my fidgeting fingers.

"I'm going to find out who he is," says Henry. There's an urgent quality to his words. "At least we know who hired him."

I flinch at the memory of the man's face and the sound of his feet behind me. I am still shaking at the realization someone wanted to kill me. If Henry hadn't come, I would have been just a nameless body, lifeless and pale, found on the sidewalk.

"I don't—I don't understand," I say, reeling. "If that man came after me because of the operation, that means—"

"Only the three of us at MI6 know about what happened in Warsaw and how it's connected. Emerson hired him; there's no other explanation," he states. Placing his hands over my own, I see him peer at me through blurry vision. "I'm so sorry, Amara. I know how much Emerson means to you."

I shove off from the sofa, wrapping my arms around my own waist. I mourn what this means: that Emerson is not only involved but, in an effort to rid himself of any liabilities, has put my life in danger. This can't be like Warsaw. I cannot continue to deny or resist the violent evidence. Emerson's betrayal, if never personal for him, has become wholly personal for me. It lances me between my shoulder blades like a knife to the back.

"Let me put a kettle on." Henry stands, gesturing to the kitchen.

I turn. "This is not an occasion for tea, you Brit. Get me something stronger." I make a move toward the kitchen, but he shoos me away.

"I'll do it. It was a cut to my arm, not my legs."

"Just be brisk about it," I say wryly, taking a seat and pointing to the cupboard above the sink. "You're bleeding everywhere."

Henry gives me a grin. A minute later, we're wincing from the sharp burn of gin. He leans back into the sofa. He's still pressing the cloth against his arm, though he's hardly bleeding now. Wrapping it tightly with a mesh bandage, he checks the tightness. Tossing the towel, his eyes follow mine to the table.

"Bleach should get it out without any issue."

"Don't worry," I say between sips, "anything you've touched I'm tossing into an incinerator anyway."

"A shame, I'm fond of this chair."

He runs a hand along the cushion beneath him. The hand movement sparks a memory like a wildfire: kissing right here a year before, the memory of his warm hands rising closer to the *V* of my thighs. I look away.

"Why were you following me?" I ask, though I'm not mad at him for it.

"You were angry with me. I was... worried," he says, looking away. "I had only planned on making sure you got inside."

"It would have had a very different outcome if you hadn't gone after me," I say with a hard swallow. "I'm truly grateful."

He seems more surprised by my appreciation than by the sight of that man with the knife. With a heavy sigh, he pours another splash of gin into my glass, then his. The tips of our fingers brush as he hands me my drink. Outside, the streets below are a distant noise from the floor of my flat. The Tower Bridge is a quiet star in the distance. The earlier downpour has scattered across the sidewalks below, a reflective mirror of the starless night. Between my adrenaline rush and the gin, the evening view brings in a rush of normalcy.

"Remind me never to get into a fight with you," I tell him.

He gives me a side eye. "Remind me never to get into a fight with *you*."

"Moi?" I indicate to myself innocently. "But I'm as tender as a kitten."

He snorts. "Only a kitten with claws would try to convince you of not having any."

"Speaking of, I want to learn defensive moves," I tell him sincerely. "Like what you did tonight."

He studies me over his glass. "Seriously?"

"Dead serious."

"Might be a bit soon, I think," he says, and for some reason, we both chortle at that, the morbidity of it. It releases a tightness in my chest, like sucking air back into my lungs.

When we've each caught our breath, he says, "All right. If you want to learn defensive strategies, the first line of defense is awareness. The second is practice."

I stand, pulling the coffee table to the side and out of the way. The rug beneath my bare feet is soft. It was harder to be irritated with him when he saved my life, and when there's gin.

"Let's practice."

To his credit, he doesn't give me any looks of incredulity, nor any wordless look of, *Right now, are you kidding me?* He sets his drink on the table, and we're face-to-face.

"In order to think like an agent, you must behave like one. To be able to hear things, you have to allow yourself to blend in and remain unforgettable."

The shape of his dark eyes scan me. I try to picture him out in the field, and even witnessing him earlier, I still can't. I understand acutely, in a way I haven't before, that he has put himself at risk many times in his career. All in the name of protecting his country. The nameless, faceless people in this country who would never know who he is or what he does. It has been muscle memory to spurn his coquettish behavior, though now that I think of it, he's only been that way toward me. I tuck away the part of me that has always spurned him. It's not the thanks he deserves—at least for tonight. I don't make promises, but as we stand in my living room, my gratitude takes hold of my attention by small degrees, an unfamiliar thing that begins to grow tentacles.

"I'll show you a few moves for various circumstances," he says.

With ease and purpose, he demonstrates several defensive countermeasures: one for being caught with an arm around my throat, a few for forced proximity, one meant to create distance, and another for the best method of gouging eyes. His hands are strong, calloused, as they place mine on his body with instruction. But after three glasses, I'm a giggling mess. I'd be more embarrassed if he weren't also laughing, bending at the waist. He straightens with a laugh, hardly in better shape.

"Perhaps another time, without that," he says, pointing to the half-full bottle.

"Then how will I endure my time with you?"

His lips curl, but he gives no response.

"Why is it you never argue with me or throw something equally hostile my way?" I ask, with an accompanying hiccup.

"You ask as if you wish I would."

"Only to know you are indeed human."

He lowers to the floor, and I find myself lowering beside him. I can feel his body heat even as we face the view of the city, our feet pointed toward the windows. It would nearly be romantic if it weren't for the bloody cloth and the bandage and our history and my unyielding hate of him. Except for those things, of course.

"It's easy to antagonize you." The fabric of his shirt rustles as he shrugs. "And anyway, I like a woman who can insult me to my face."

"Something is wrong with you," I say matter-of-factly, tipping my head back to finish the last of what's in my glass. I turn to find his eyes fastening on mine.

"Most definitely," he said. Shadows trace his jaw, and his expression takes on an impassive look. "Are you going to tell me why you were so upset earlier? You seemed ready for a fight when you got to Taro."

My smile fades. I shift my eyes toward the view out the window. What was the harm in cracking open my chest, just this one time? What was real anyway, in the dark?

"There was some bad news." I twist sideways, resting my arm on the seat of the sofa to look at him. "Do you remember when I told you about my visit to Warsaw?"

"The children's home, right?"

I give a nod. "I wasn't able to talk to anyone at the time. No one knew much about who left me there." My eyes turn, tracing the shape of faraway buildings in the distance. "But a woman who used to work at the home called me. She was there the night my birth mother left me. Apparently—" I meet his eyes. "She told me my mother died the day after I was left. Some horrible car crash or another that was in the news."

"In Warsaw?"

"Yes," I say. "The woman who called me is convinced my mother's death was more than accidental."

"Why does she think that?" He tilts his head toward me.

"She said my mother had been afraid for me, and leaving me at that home in Warsaw was her way of trying to keep me safe," I tell him with a wavering breath. Maybe it's because I have long stopped caring what he thinks that I find myself saying the truth aloud. "I suppose I… It's taken me by surprise how affected I am. Ridiculous, right? It was such a long time ago."

Henry doesn't offer false assurances. "But she's your mother," he says. "There's never enough time for that to make itself right."

I am overcome by his sudden use of the present tense. The words form an endless loop; *she's your mother, she's your mother, she's your mother.*

Every parent I should have loved for a lifetime is gone. It's terrifying how love keeps slipping through my fingers. What would I do if I had a child and if they were in danger? What would be the things I wish I could say if I had very little time to say them? I think of my mother, this faceless woman who might have saved me from some worse fate… Was the act of leaving me, in fact, a blessing in disguise? And if she was protecting me from someone, then who?

I want to turn into something cutting, a living scythe sharp enough to fight off death. I want to tell Henry all of these things because maybe he understands what it is to be alone, too, but the words are frozen in my throat. If he notices my rumination, he doesn't say anything. In the dim light of the room, the silhouette of his profile is in stark contrast to the glimmering night out my window. I wish I could just say it: I'm tired of life feeling so solitary. I don't believe that love should solve everything, but with him, it was the closest I'd been to it in a long time. As I close my door behind him that night, I know I must deserve to be alone. After all, why else would so many people leave?

Chapter Twenty

London, England, Three weeks later

A light knock at my office door draws my attention away from the red-lined document in my hand. Expecting Madeline, I'm surprised to see Tobias standing at the door instead. I set aside the brief I'm working on.

"I'm heading out," he says with a smile. "I'll see you at the Gala?"

While I want to be honest and say, *I'm full of regrets that I committed to going*, and also, *I've six dresses and hate them all*, I return his smile and instead reply, "I'll be there."

"Excellent. I'll be the one in a black tux," he says with a wave. He walks out, bidding goodbye to those still in the office. Since that night at the pub, he's been friendlier, though the ease of conversations comes and goes. Sometimes, I can't tell what his interest is—whether it's professional or something more. There's a lack of charm to him that I find interesting, if different.

I take a few more minutes to wrap up before I lock the document in my desk drawer and grab my bag. There's random chatter in the open space of the office as I pass through, everyone distracted by conversations of tomorrow evening's soiree. Henry's standing between Madeline and another woman. I'm only sort of familiar with her, though she's on another team in the cyber division. She has delicate features, wavy blonde hair slung halfway over her shoulder, and an easy smile. From this distance, the smile he's giving her is like a stake into my gut. Turning, I throw my light coat over an arm and duck out of sight before anyone spots me. As I head toward the lift, I hear a ping from inside my bag. The soft chime of the lift indicates its arrival, and I step inside. Leaning against a handrail, I read the text from James.

I have some last-minute details to review for a case. Top secret, you know (because I'm very, very important). Get together next week after your fancy black tie thing?

I'm smiling to myself and thinking of a response when suddenly Henry is there, stepping in just in time before the doors of the lift close. His eyes glance at the phone in my hands. The weight of his invisible curiosity hangs in the air, though I pretend not to notice.

"You again." I lean back against the wall and return my phone to my bag. Since that night after Taro, he somehow always finds me as I'm leaving the office. There's a buzzing beneath my skin whenever he's around. There's nothing rational about it. I had convinced myself that our affair last year was nothing—a fling that came and went. I had moved past it. Memories I had stowed away have become unearthed again, memories of his hands pressing against me, inside me. Then I think of a few weeks before, the rain and his eyes and the taste of gin and the brush of his body warm next to mine, sitting on the floor. As if I am bracing for a storm on a ship, it's been hard to find my footing.

He crosses his legs as we descend. "I've only seen you smile like that when I'm pushing your buttons."

"It's only James." I roll my eyes.

"A lucky chap."

I can't help it, I throw my head back with a laugh. His eyes watch me, an unreadable expression across his face.

"James is harmless," I say. "Not a very good flirt, for one."

"Is he as much of a prick as Tobias?" he asks with a scowl.

"He's not a prick," I tell him with a quirk of a brow. "And honestly, neither is Tobias. He's okay, really."

"Now *that's* a laugh," replies Henry. He glances at the blinking red arrow indicating our descent. "So, tomorrow?"

I play dumb. "Is there something going on?"

He eyes me, trying to figure out if I'm playing or not. "If you need convincing, I'll be wearing a suit."

These men and their bloody suits.

"That's nice," I say with a shrug. "For you."

"You're not going?"

"I never said that." We're nearing the ground floor now, and I shift my bag to my other hand.

"Do you get something out of torturing me?" he asks, not really a question.

The doors open wide. Through a half-hidden smile, I say to him over my shoulder, "It's always a bonus."

Chapter Twenty-One

Somewhere outside of London

I peer out the car window as a sprawling estate comes into view. Its style reminds me of country homes I've seen scattered throughout the UK, though at a much grander scale. Dusk is a shade of golden apricot glinting above each palatial spiral on the roof, a half-dozen chimneys crowning the roof for tonight's event. The driver slowly follows the curve of the gravel drive around a large fountain, a line of brake lights ahead of us. The gala was planned with the presence of the entire agency in mind. By the number of people walking inside, it appears many are indeed in attendance. A good thing, then, that this country home seems to come with enough rooms and elegance fit for the prime minister. Given how many of us from MI6 are in attendance, security is tight, and I spot men on the roof monitoring the scene below.

We've been waiting for a few minutes. With another glance from the backseat, I'm not optimistic that waiting in the car is the best solution.

"Here is fine," I say to the driver, pushing open the door, "Thank you."

Taking a deep inhale of the fresh air, I begin to make my way to the entrance. I notice a wrap-around garden. Far enough outside of London, the air lingers along my bare shoulders. I ascend the stairs flanked by large, rectangular windows. The silk of my dress swishes softly, my chocolate hair twisted over my shoulder in a loose wave. The blue of my dress is cerulean. It's a shade deeper than the salty sea of the Atlantic, though the fabric causes an emulating effect of undulating waves as I walk. A miracle at all that I was finally able to settle on what to wear, given that I was in a state of mind not to come at all. Crowds and small talk have a lethal effect on my interest in socializing. I tell myself I only need to stay for an hour or two. I'll show my face, then leave when everyone is a few glasses in. No one will notice I'm gone until I'm already halfway to my flat.

Staff holding trays of champagne offer glasses as I and other guests trickle through the door. It's easy to admire the grandness of the manor, given how much goes into running it. I accept a champagne glass from a staff member holding a silver tray, and walk into a large drawing room where the gala is being held. Orchestral music plays from the corners of the room. No one is dancing, but people are lingering in front of the food. I keep an eye out for anyone I recognize, my hair swinging as I look from side to side. A group standing to my left shifts, and in the space where they'd been is Henry.

I see him with a few others, standing in a black suit and bow tie. My eyes trace over him without him noticing. His right hand is casually loose in his pocket while the other hand brings a glass filled with amber liquid up to his lips. I want to lick the taste of it from his mouth. My heart slams inside my chest, a dull and heavy weight against skin and bones. I want him... again?

No, that's not right. I want him *still*. Perhaps I never, ever stopped wanting him. I just became good at convincing myself I didn't.

The five-second head start of seeing him first gives me time to gather myself. By the time his head swivels my way, I've cooled my features to hide the tingling sensation at my neck when our eyes meet. My champagne is half-gone, and the base of the glass is resting lightly in my palm. When Nora catches sight of me, she waves. A few others turn to look, and then I have no choice but to say hello. Returning her wave, I take a deep breath and make my way over. As I get closer, I see the woman from the office earlier, and she's saying something into Henry's ear, her hand resting delicately on his forearm. He's looking past her in my direction. My stomach dips. There's an intensity there that nearly fumbles the smile I fixed on my face.

"You look *so* lovely," says Nora before I can get out a word, but she says it so earnestly that from anyone else it would ring sarcastic. "You match the elegance of the house—" she says, gesturing to the ornate ceiling, the gilded frames, the plush carpet.

"That's very kind," I reply with a shy kind of laugh. "As do you."

"When I first heard it would be here, I was skeptical any of us would clean up properly," says Nora as she plucks a glass of champagne off a moving tray. "It's such a nice occasion to dress up for once."

"I love this!" Madeline sweeps into the conversation and gives me a warm embrace with very little notice. "You've outshone all of us."

I motion to shush Madeline, but Nora is nodding vigorously in agreement. Nora's husband comes up and introduces himself to the group of us, including Piper—whose name I finally remember—and they're making bets about how many rooms there are in the manor. Two others from the cyber team chime in, and I can feel Henry's attention, so I throw out an arbitrary number as I continue to evade meeting his gaze. In the corner of my eye, I see movement as he heads toward the drink table. It isn't until I glance over that I realize Piper is pulling him forward by the hand.

I try to appear like I'm listening, but I don't deny myself a second glass of champagne to hide my smile stretching as taut as a live wire. What does it matter if she's touching him? I have no claim to him. Wouldn't, even if I was given the chance.

As the night continues, conversations become a revolving game of musical chairs. The room becomes more crowded with people and pleasantries, champagne, and toffee tarts. Eventually, I find myself in a group along with Tobias and Emerson, and a few are arguing the merits of playing rugby at a young age. I try to keep up, but truthfully, I've lost count of the number of champagne glasses I've had, as well as everything else.

"—I'm saying leadership is only half of it," says Aaron, an agent from Ireland, if I recall correctly. "Think of the children who look up to a lad like Josh Doris, it's good to have idols—"

"He is indeed one of the best," adds another colleague, whose name I think is Archer, or maybe Augustus or something similarly pretentious, nodding in agreement. "I used to have a poster of him up in my room as a kid."

"Rugby can't have been the reason you came all this way," says Tobias with a smile. His warmth surprises me, and I smile back.

"I can't say it was," I say with a laugh.

"Are you having a nice time?" He gestures around us.

I'm tipsy enough not to hide my feelings at first instinct. My attempt to cover it is clumsy. "It's—nice." I look around. "Especially the art on the walls."

"It's okay," he says with a chuckle. "No one has a gun to your head. You can be honest."

A warm blush rises up my neck. I decide the glass in my hand is the last one for the evening. "It's been a nice time, really. Though I also won't mind being at home after this," I reveal. "A good thing is there's a day between the party and Monday."

"What do you normally do on the weekends?" he asks.

"I read, go to the cinema," I say with a shrug. "Same as everyone."

Tobias gives me a long, studying look. "Are you seeing anyone?"

The personal nature of his question takes me by surprise. "Ah, no. I'm really flattered, Tobias, but I'm not—it's not like that for me."

"What?" he asks with a laugh that makes me second-guess the intent behind his question. "I'm not asking for me. Personally, I'm not remotely looking for that kind of thing. I was only making conversation." At his second laugh, seemingly filled with amusement by my assumption, I suddenly felt the heat of embarrassment. Maybe I'd come off as self-absorbed by assuming he was asking for me.

"I... It's not a yes or no for me." I see Henry standing across the room and look away. "It's complicated."

"Things seem to only get more complicated the older we get, eh?" Says Tobias. I give a nod, then immediately freeze when I see Henry making his way toward us, weaving through the room. He's only a dozen steps away. Panic ensues. I'm surely a bit tipsy; I can't trust myself like this right now.

Fortunately, I am saved by the perfume and splash of champagne that is Madeline and Nora.

"Did you know there's a fortune teller in the other room?" Asks Madeline gleefully. "The agency finally footed the bill for something *useful* for once."

They laugh and drag me along with them as Henry steps into the place where I was, and I have no objections. Having been in the same spot most of the evening, the red velvet curtains and intricate paintings match the decadence of the former room. There's only one person in line, and as soon as they're done, the three of us sit at the table. The dark lavender cloth reads, *Palmistry by Prynath.* A small bottle of hand sanitizer rests on the table, mostly out of sight.

"We're here for a reading," says Madeline with all the confidence of someone who has drank too much. "I have things to learn."

One by one, Prynath reads our palms for a few minutes each. Madeline goes first, listening as she's given reassuring guidance on the rest of her year, as well as a possible influx of creativity if she can reign in her impulsiveness. Unperturbed, Madeline nods her head in rapid agreement. Nora listens fixedly as she's told, "The wish you've been waiting for will happen after the full moon in December."

I stifle a laugh, certain that it's either a baby or a posh car. When Prynath turns to hold my outstretched hand, her dark, almond eyes gradually narrow.

"Hmm..." she says.

"Hmm?"

She doesn't look up, only traces a finger along the longer curve of my right hand. "May I?" she asks, pointing to my left. I watch as she studies the slope of lines in my other hand.

"Find anything interesting?" I say with a joking smile.

"Your life will soon change dramatically," she says. "And do you see here? This is your heart line, and this one is the line for your mind. They are very deep, which means you are always conflicted with which should rule you."

I arch a brow at the dubious wisdom she's imparting. "Fascinating."

Her head ducks downward to trace another line, her dark hair falling around her face. "You will have a very interesting life, full of surprises. You will marry, and there will be danger." Her pinky follows along another groove in my hand. "This line tells me you are rational, though melancholy." She lifts her head, her dark hair sweeping across the surface of the table. "You have had a lot of sadness in your life. You will have an opportunity for happiness soon, if you let yourself."

A cold sensation chills down my spine as if someone has run an ice cube along it. I withdraw my hand, rubbing my fingertips along the lines she'd traced. Madeline and Nora watch me rise, worried expressions on their faces. They walk with me as we leave the table. I glance over my shoulder, and the woman's eyes follow mine. I turn away.

Nora touches my arm as we walk into the other room. "Are you all right? She was strange."

"Jesus Christ, doesn't she know you're to keep things light and *fun* at a party?" Madeline grumbles, though I know she's only doing so on my behalf.

I can't tell if the alcohol has started to wear off or if the encounter sobered me up. The elegance of the house transforms into something heavier, almost oppressive. My heart squeezes in my chest as the crowd pushes in around us. I want to flee.

I halt. "I'm all right," I say with a forced smile. "Really. I can tell you I've had enough to drink, though. I'll just run to the loo."

They don't follow after me as I make my way out the ornate double doors, my heels echoing in the quiet of the hallway. My fingers are still pressing into my palm with a trembling pressure, my nails digging into my skin so deeply they seek to undo the lines that have proven to a stranger what I thought only I could see in myself.

Chapter Twenty-Two

Turning a corner, the party becomes a vague thrum of music and laughter in the distance. It's a relief to be alone after the past few hours of socializing. Now that I'm calmer, I wish I'd reacted differently. I hate feeling manipulated, but no matter how much I intellectualize it, I know I should have simply laughed it off. Regret is an unpleasant weight, dragging like shackles at my feet as I wander further into the house. My hand glides along the length of the hallway until there's nowhere else to go.

Here, the hall's wainscoting is a stark ivory against velvet-red curtains. Curious, I open each door and inspect the rooms, though I'm not really looking for anything. There's only more velvet, chandeliers, and luxurious rugs. I come across a large room with curtains drawn apart. Walking gingerly inside, I can see moonlight gleaming in a cloudless night. I remove my heels and let my bare feet sink into the intricate floral designs of the carpet. Moving to sit on the built-in window seat, I peer up at the moon. The plush carpet absorbs the sound of my shoes when I drop them on the floor one at a time. The view out the window faces the front fountain of the estate and the gravel drive where I had been dropped off earlier.

Country homes have a ridiculous amount of space. Despite each uninhabited room I've found, envy is an unflattering spike in my chest. What would it be like to live in a place like this? To make a home in the country where I can breathe in fresh air, walk in the garden, and stand beneath blooming trees? London has been good for my career, but as more time passes, I can admit to myself, here in the dark, that I secretly wish for something different. What would it feel like to make a home in a place far from the city?

"There's a cardinal sin about Irish goodbyes when you're not in Ireland."

My head turns to the voice at the door. Henry is standing in the half-dark, watching me. He's leaning his shoulder against the frame, ankles crossed. I turn away.

"Of course, you're here," I say with an edge to my voice. " It was so peaceful. Is there a signal that goes off when I'm having a nice time?"

His footfalls grow closer. He stands a few feet from the window, his knees meeting the soft cushion of the window seat. I can smell whiskey and vetiver.

"The moon is lovely tonight," he comments.

"It was lovelier alone."

"Is that true?"

"Fine. I was indulgently playing the world's tiniest violin. Now go away."

"But I'm enjoying the view."

"Aren't you expected elsewhere?" I say as I point out the door, impatience sweeping through me.

"Where?" He quirks a brow, inviting himself to sit at an arm's length on the cushion. "By whom?"

"Piper, what's her face, or whatever."

"Ah, so it's *jealousy* that's making you so sullen. I've never seen this side of you before." He gives me a roguish smile.

"I'm *sullen* because you're impeding on my solitude," I tell him with a glare.

"So you say."

A beat of silence.

"Are you going to leave?"

"Only if you admit you're jealous."

"Can you ever just let something go?" I say as scathingly as possible. Maybe now he'll finally listen.

"Ah," he says with amusement. "So you're irritated because I'm right."

Expelling a breath of exasperation, I give him a side eye until I notice the top button of his shirt is undone. A pang of desire scoops out onto my tongue, and I swallow, returning my focus to the world outside as a distraction.

"Hardly."

"I know you think you want to be left alone, but you don't," he says. "Not really."

I snort. "Pardon, what is it you think you know about me?"

"You're like a cat, you just like to know someone else is around—"

"That wasn't an actual invitation to talk."

He lets out a sigh. "Fine, if you want to have a row, let's have a proper row then—"

"No!" I say in a sharp whisper, eyes darting to the empty hallway. "Anyway, I have nothing to say to you."

"No, no, let's finally have it out, Amara. We'll both feel better for it." His voice is deep, low. He leans toward me with a tight expression, forearms pressing on his thighs. His eyes are darker than the shadows that loom in every corner. I realize he's... frustrated. It dials up the focus of his expression, which is directed at me. It coils around my waist like a grip.

"It's just us here. Have a real go at me so you can admit how you feel, and we can stop dancing around it." He stands, pacing. "Clearly, you're still angry about last fall. Are you also angry about tonight because you saw me with another woman and assumed it must mean something? Tell me that you're not still drawn to me, too; tell me that you haven't felt some kind of regret from walking away from what we had—"

"—I have nothing to regret!" I argue. I rise from my seat, my index finger pointing at his chest with hostility. "*I'm* not the one who lied. You are. You're a ridiculous womanizer, and I am right not to trust you."

"Perhaps instead of making assumptions, you can finally let me explain myself to you, and apologize again—"

"I have two eyes," I scoff. "You and I both know you were with someone else while we were together. There's nothing to explain, because there's nothing to *fix*. After this operation, I want nothing to do with you anymore."

"If you would just listen, goddammit, I'm trying to say I should have told you before. It was for a case. I realize now how that must have felt for you to see me with someone—"

"Who gives a shit about beforehand!" I hiss. Reliving it aloud with him burns in my chest. My anger and sorrow become something monstrous inside me, taking on a life of their own. "You shouldn't have lied to me from the start! Do you understand how hard it is for me to trust people? Did you really think everything could be the same after that? Do you understand what this operation has done to me since you told me about Emerson? It has thoroughly fucked with my head. I don't need you fucking with it further!"

His eyes harden. "Of course, I know it would affect you. I know you have difficulty trusting people, and I even understand why. But you shut me out without hesitation. You never gave me a chance to understand or explain. How do I know you weren't looking for the first opportunity to do so? How do I know you weren't already looking for an out?" He puts one foot in front of the other, advancing toward me, an animal prowling in the dark. "It's also one thing to be upset with me because you assume I was with another woman out of enjoyment—*which I wasn't*—and it's another to outright deny the part of my career I have been dealing with long before you came into my life. You've been quite blind to the fact that I want to *protect* you, not *hurt* you."

Something about his words snaps into splinters in my chest, and

I whirl on him. "I don't need your protection."

Henry takes three strides to the door, where he shuts it with an incongruous gentleness. He rounds on me.

"It has *never* been my intention to hurt you, Amara—"

"Stop saying my goddamn name!"

He stops talking, his hands going up like a white flag calling for a truce. Moonlight slants across his face. I'm heaving breaths, feeling like I could breathe fire. In my chest, I feel an ache of everything we've said to one another. For several moments, our gaze locks.

Henry lowers his hands. "I am so sorry, all right? I would do it all so differently if I could," he says, his mouth taut. His voice casts a long shadow of bitterness in the quiet of the room. "What was happening between us was so new that the messiness of my career hadn't yet caught up to it. So I get it, all right? You want to protect yourself, but what I wish I had done right the first time was show you that *I* want to protect you, too." He's watching me, and says carefully, "You're so afraid to get hurt, I don't think you've considered that perhaps it's you who's going to ruin me."

My eyes suddenly burn with emotion, and I face away from him so he can't see. I have run out of steam, my ire evaporating. I'm not sure if it's from the rush of adrenaline or the shadows, but honesty finds its way out of my beating heart into the room.

"After you saved my life, I thought it would be easier to forgive you, but it's harder now. It feels like there's more at stake. I understand your job is unconventional, and I understand what it means for you. But I'm so terrified of where that puts me. We were supposed to be something different, something that lasted. All our fallout did was confirm that good things always end for me," I say, my voice thick. Turning, I look him in the eyes.

"We'll do things differently if you give us another chance," he says softly. The dark of his irises glint from every ounce of light in the room. "I can ask to be removed from operations that would require any kind of relationship front. And I'm not only telling you I can make promises. I'll prove it to you."

Surprise slowly massages the tension out of my shoulders. Do I trust him? Will I ever be able to trust him again? Is it worth the risk?

He takes a step forward. "You know, I wanted to hold you the moment I saw you in this dress tonight."

Releasing my arms at my side, I let myself dip into the intoxication of his gaze. He steps closer, his voice husky.

"I've always wanted to dance with you."

"Would have drawn more attention tonight than it'd be worth," I say, thinking of the crowded room.

He lifts a hand toward mine. "If I can't dance with you out there, I'll dance with you here in the dark."

I consider resisting, but truthfully, I don't want to. When he reaches for me, I hand myself over to him with a warm palm. Our bodies meet, warm and sure and familiar. He's a head taller, and it's almost too easy to rest a cheek against his chest. We dance slowly in place. Silvery light slopes across his cheek. We can't hear any chatter or any music. We're only dancing together as if there's some invisible string guiding us in tandem.

"You're a better dancer than I thought," I admit.

He pulls back to look at me. "Was that an actual compliment?"

"Not now that you've ruined it." I duck my head to hide a smile.

The fission where our hands meet imperceptibly evolves as we continue dancing. The curves of my waist are warm beneath his hand, and slowly, it urges me forward. He's looking at me like how he used to, with total and completely unguarded affection.

"You're stunning," he breathes. His lips lower to my shoulder, pressing a tender kiss against the skin there. I'm tired of talking myself out of what I want simply because I think I don't deserve it.

Rising on the balls of my feet, I drag my mouth upwards, and he's already halfway there. He covers my mouth with his. I break open in his arms. Our kiss builds with a longing neither of us had forgotten. How did I ever convince myself I could forget what this feels like? I want him. Of course I do. I have always wanted him.

His fingertips drift up the length of my dress, and he palms my cheekbones to hold my face close. Kissing him is exactly as I remember it. His lips softly part as his tongue slips inside. A stampede of zoo animals could run in, and we wouldn't break apart. I want mouthfuls of him, all the air in his lungs, and more.

It takes me a few moments to realize he's walking me backwards. He moves us into a small alcove, shielded from view and out of sight from the door. My hands push off his jacket. His hand slides under my thigh and pulls my leg to wrap it around him. When the first slender finger of his traces up my dress and slides inside, I shiver against him. With deft fingers, he pulls aside the fabric and touches the soft, wet center of me. I gasp into his mouth. His tongue traces over mine as he begins to move. I tilt my head back, panting. His teeth skim along the pulse at my neck, and I can't think. Pressing into the heel of his palm, I ride the pleasure of it like a tide, letting it drag me into its deeper waters. He holds me tight as he slips another finger in. I whisper breathlessly, over and over, *more, deeper, right there, please*.

When I say his name, he looks at me with hooded lids as if he might devour me completely then and there. The spark we had lit between us last fall is now a fuse, igniting us. I'd welcome it. So that there's no room for uncertainty, I use both hands to slide my panties until they're all the way to the floor. I step out of them.

"I want it to be here." I reach for him. "I don't want to wait."

I'm not leaving much room for argument, but he doesn't seem to need very much convincing. The rough unfastening of his zipper sounds, and his pants falling to the floor follow. I let out a shudder of anticipation, watching him hold himself in his hand, pumping himself once, twice. Our eyes meet as he nears, stepping between my legs as I part them. I bunch the silk fabric of my dress in one hand and grip his arm with the other. With the feel of the silk-smooth head of his cock sliding into the wet center of me, I gasp. All the control I've held onto these past months snaps, like a leash, like a whip against the soft flesh of my skin. My back arches against the wall as he presses into me. This is the kind of ecstasy that eclipses all other pleasures. The airless sensation of handing myself over to gratification. I'd believed my intensity toward him had been guided by betrayal, a ferocity of emotion that had twisted over time. Its malformed shape was a passionate lie. There's no hiding from each other now, not now in this primal state. His eyes fix on mine in the dim light, naked, revealing, full of reverence. All this time, I thought he wanted nothing from me. But his eyes say something else. They say, *I want everything.* I want to give him everything.

Our moans fill the room as he slowly, slowly inches forward. I'm impatient. Undulating my hips, I seek the full length of him to take what I want. He leans his forehead on mine as he brings himself closer in that final inch. Wetting his thumb on this tongue, he lowers it gently to the most sensitive part of me. All my life, I have shunned anything warm until all that was left was a cold room. As his mouth drags across my neck, as he holds me at the waist and presses deeper, I'm certain I'm not cold anymore.

Chapter Twenty-Three

London, England, One month later

"You look... cheerful," says Henry as I open the door to my flat. I turn on my heel and return to the kitchen counter. Behind me, I hear the click of the latch and a rustle from his coat as he hangs it on a hook by the door.

"Are you cooking?"

"I'm flossing, clearly." Measuring out another cup of flour, I dump it into a large mixing bowl.

"No lessons tonight?" he asks, referring to the self-defense moves he's been teaching me.

"Not tonight. I thought we could mix it up," I say.

He sidles up next to me, observing my handiwork. I glance at him. One brow raises inquisitively in my direction.

"We could get takeaway. My treat."

"Stop provoking me," I say with a twinge of irritation, "I'm trying to focus."

I re-read the recipe in the book, my finger pointing at each ingredient, and mutter under my breath, "...If the butter was first before the step to sauté, that means the ordinal position for the vegetables is..."

I know Henry is watching me. My eyes dart to my periphery, then back to the cookbook. "What?"

"Nothing," he says, giving a skeptical look toward the page. "Carry on."

Continuing, I read the instructions twice to ensure I don't miss anything. "I think I need to Brunoise the carrots next."

"All right, now you're just making up words."

I ignore him. Within a few minutes, I realize I've accidentally mixed up the ingredients. It was a cup of sugar, not flour. My stomach flips as his long body presses into me.

Henry's hands softly begin to roam over my hips, pulling me in. Suddenly, I'm being lifted onto the countertop next to the measuring cup and uncut vegetables. The handle of the cupboard digs into my back, though I hardly care.

"We're going to make a mess," I say.

There's a wicked glint in his eye. "Precisely."

"All right, you libertine," I say, letting out a laugh. "We're in a kitchen, have you no moral fiber?"

His lips press on the sensitive spot above my clavicle.

"As if you aren't turned on by my naughty principles."

"You are a bit. Though there are other words I'd use," I say, my words coming out breathy as his mouth traces downward. His fingers begin to unbutton my pants.

He pauses. "Such as?"

"Obstinate." A teasing smile splits my lips. "Obsessed."

"It's true that I am, but only about you." His fingertips graze my ankle.

"Let's not forget, a complete tosser," I improvise.

"Oh?" he asks, pulling back to look at me. "Is that really how you'd describe me?"

"Do you mean, if I were forced to admit I knew you?"

He discards my pants on the floor of the kitchen and takes a step back to admire me. On his knees, his lips graze the inside of my thigh. His breath is hot along my skin. He tongues me over sheer fabric. My hands find their way into his hair, pressing him closer. The heat of his mouth unfurls all the desire I've been keeping at an arm's reach. I reach for it, for him, now. I'll never get enough of this.

Later, he's kissing me at the door. "I don't want to leave," his voice in a low whisper.

I press my mouth to his neck, and once again to his lips.

"All the more reason to come back," I say.

Only until after Henry's left do I realize I don't give him enough credit. Part of his cleverness is the useful skill of knowing how to successfully distract. I never even finished dinner.

Chapter Twenty-Four

London, England, One month later

I dim all the lights in the flat and crawl into bed. Henry's arms open, welcoming me. It's late, but I don't want to fall asleep yet.

"Tell me something about you," I say softly. "Something no one else knows."

His fingers trace circles on my wrist as he thinks. Propping himself up, he reaches for his phone.

"It's understood that an alias I use will be thoroughly vetted by any groups I'm infiltrating," he says, tapping his screen. "So it's crucial to maintain certain norms, like social media profiles. Having an online presence means maintaining a facade. It's important to show an interest in something real."

My stomach tightens. What is he about to show me? His eyes follow mine as he hands me his phone. I frown, scrolling through and tapping a few times to look at different settings in his profile.

He shifts to see what's on the screen. "Wait—what are you looking at?"

There's a series of videos; I scroll to the fifth or sixth one until I find the most severe example. I turn the screen to face him. A cheery song plays while a mini Aussie does zoomies around a dog park. The next is an ASMR video of a bunny being fed carrots.

"I don't know," I say gravely, "this seems more like blackmail material than support for an alias."

He laughs, sinking into the bed again. I hand him back his phone. With a thoughtful expression, he asks me, "Did you ever grow up with pets?"

I shake my head. "My adopted parents were allergic. Friends who had pets seemed to really like them, but I've always felt pretty neutral about it. You?"

"My mother was allergic to cats," he says with a laugh. "For some reason, that never stopped her from keeping two of them."

"No one keeps cats," I joke, "I'm fairly certain they keep people as pets."

"That sounds like something my father would say." He wears a loose smile, pulling the covers over his hips. He is the vision of a man at ease. "He grew up in Korea and used to rescue cats when he was young."

I prop my head on my hand. "Where do your parents live?" Pausing, I blink. "Or—sorry, is that okay to know?"

"Of course," he says. "Not much to know, though, they both passed away. My mother first, then my father. I think he was too heartbroken to keep going on without her."

"That's so... sad."

Turning to face me, he rests his palm against his temple, but there's a faraway look in his eyes. "It was. But I get it—they were very close. There was this thing my father used to say sometimes, after my mother would return from running errands or taking a trip. He'd greet her and say, '*Tu étais où pendant tout ce temps?*'"

Furrowing my brow, I look at him expectantly.

"It means, 'where have you been all my life?'" He explains.

"Your father spoke French, too?"

"Not at first. But my mother did, so he learned. My mother used to tell me how much she loved that he did that." Henry pulls me in, his chest warm as I rest my cheek against him. His fingertips gently trace the scar from Warsaw along my temple. "She said he made her feel like home wasn't only a country, but also a person."

Chapter Twenty-Five

London, England, One month later

Half an hour after a meeting with Emerson, I'm pacing my flat. When the lock to my door rustles, I look up to see Henry walking in. He shuts the door with a grim expression.

"What are we going to do?" I ask, barely able to tamp down my panic. "If the fob in Japan destroyed the test device, how will we know it will work on the real thing? This is so *fucked*."

"We can do another test, have another fob coded similarly with a self-destruction component," he says. His expression tells me he's just as concerned, but his voice is level, collected. He's under a lot more pressure and is far better at hiding it than I can. "We've still had success. With Antoni's intel, we found that bomb ahead of it going off."

I wring my hands. "They're always two steps ahead," I say helplessly. "We're trying to prevent them from doing anything resembling Warsaw, and this fob was supposed to be the key. Is there no way Antoni can try and get the access key—"

"We've talked about this," he says with a sigh. "It's a risk to Antoni's life that won't end with us getting what we want. It has to be this way."

A sudden contemplative look crosses his face.

"What?" I ask.

"What if we..." he drifts off.

I wait, rain pelting against the window.

"Say we take a risk, give it to Emerson, and utilize agency resources. We don't want him to get suspicious, but if he thinks we're delaying things on purpose, he'll ask for the device outright. Then it's literally *out of our hands*. If we pivot our suggestion to bringing it to him, we can at least control some of the terms and be there when it's accessed."

"I thought the entire point of doing this was to avoid having the device brought to the agency?" I point out. "That if Emerson isn't the only one betraying the agency, that information could get into the wrong hands just as easily. If that happened, it would be...."

"Disastrous," he says with a sigh. "It could undo most of the work we've done, especially after the vote on the bill in Hungary, I know. But we have to consider all possibilities. I'll need to return to Warsaw and connect with Antoni. And I think—I think it's time we talk about the safe house."

"What safe house?" I ask, my brows knitting together. "What are you talking about?"

"It's a safe house no one knows about, not even Emerson." He cups my face between his hands. "I've always had it as a possible escape hatch in case things went sideways on an op."

"How is it the service doesn't know?" I ask in puzzlement.

"It's barely an official residence," he says with a grimace. "It belonged to my French grandmother, and was the home my mother grew up in. I inherited the house after my parents passed away, and I've only been in it twice since. It's been kept under the name of my mother's trust, so it's not tied to my name in any way."

I press my palm to the outside of his hand. "You think we'll need to run?"

"Not for me. For you."

A laugh bubbles up without invitation. "You're out of your goddamn mind."

"I'm not going to enumerate again all the reasons why this operation is dangerous, and why a syndicate—who have zero qualms about killing *children*—would even hesitate to kill anyone else in their way. You are in their way."

"But I—"

He interrupts. "I'm going to pull the logic card, because there'll be no mistake in it. You are a novice. I have been an agent in the field for a decade. I will put *both* our lives in jeopardy if you are here in harm's way when there's an opportunity to leave. My only focus will be you."

I have always known drastic measures might need to be taken, but I hadn't anticipated his suggestion. How could splitting up make me safer? Worse, how do I change the mind of someone I love so deeply that I would make the same choice and do anything to make sure he's all right? I had known unforeseen possibilities would catch up to me, but the mention of a safe house where only I might go makes the air grow tight in my chest.

"It won't come to that, anyway," I say stubbornly, gripping a hand into the crook of my inner elbow. "We'll find a way to get the information from the device, and we'll have the evidence to remove Emerson. That's the right thing to happen, so it must."

He looks at me with a tender sadness that breaks my heart to see. I realize he doesn't believe the words I'm saying, and it aches.

"We'll never use the safe house," he intones. "I only want to mention it so that you know. I'll give you the details, but we'll never have to think about it after the case closes. All right?" His thumb softly grazes my lower lip. I look at him through heavy lids. The shades are halfway drawn, and the city outside gleams and winks at us in the dark. The vague shape of the iconic observation wheel shines pink along the south bank of the River Thames. Resting my cheek against his chest, I close my eyes. A moment later, Henry's hands are pulling me gently at the shoulders.

"Come to bed," he says gently. "It's late now."

I let him take me by the hand. He pulls open the pocket sliding doors and follows me into the dark of the bedroom. First, he sits me on the duvet, then removes my clothes, then both shoes. My eyes adjust to the dark and watch him as he kneels in front of me.

"How are you always so calm?" I ask. He pulls back the comforter so I can crawl into bed. "Even with all the risks?"

"It comes with the territory," he says nonchalantly. "A good agent requires a certain degree of being calm under fire, as well as being self-possessed."

I let lightness find its way back in the form of a smirk. "Or simply possessed."

His laugh breaks the tension, warming it into lingering shadows. It's a sound I want to memorize, cloak myself in when uncertainty threatens to take me under its turbulent waters. Removing his clothes, he settles in beside me. I shiver briefly at the cool air on my exposed skin. I find his mouth in the dark and press against him.

"Are you real?" He breaks off our kiss, whispering against my lips. "Sometimes I think I've made you up just to cope with the bleakness of this case. With my job. This city."

"It's real. I'm real," I say, touching his jaw tenderly with my fingertips. I wait until his eyes, pooling with emotion, meet mine in the dark. Rain beats against the windows. "Now, are you going to fuck me, or do I have to do everything myself?"

He laughs so hard he falls off the bed, dragging me onto the floor with him.

Chapter Twenty-Six

London, England, One month later

"Still jealous, I see."

I take a bite of the Indian food Henry brought for dinner. His eyes slide to mine, though he doesn't bother denying my accusation. Takeout boxes and glasses of water are strewn across the coffee table. We're sitting on the floor of the living room while London is a gray, rainy blur outside. I study him from where I sit.

"Tobias is truly harmless," I say between chews. "He doesn't flirt with me, nor does he seem interested in anything more than being friends. Also, he doesn't have a *key* to my flat." I look at him pointedly.

"Mm," Henry replies gruffly.

My spoon clatters against the edge of my bowl.

"All right, out with it."

"He pays too much attention to you." He gives me a side eye. "I don't trust it."

"That's what every man says when they can't admit they're jealous."

"Probably accurate," he says, taking a sip of water. "But it doesn't make me less right."

"I don't know if I trust that look on your face right now."

"Some thoughts can remain private, you know," he says innocently.

"You're being a bit cheeky today."

"I have something for you," he blurts out, shifting.

"If this is you trying to distract me, it's—"

He pulls a small box of matches from his pocket and rests it on my knee.

"—probably going to work," I finish. My eyebrows knit together when I notice the design on the box. It's the logo from the hotel I stayed in Poland. The hotel where I'd overheard Henry through the bathroom door, where the entire trajectory of my life changed. "Is this from Warsaw?"

"It is," he says slyly.

I open it, and with a hammering heart, I spot an inscription written beneath the matchsticks. Shaking them out into the palm of my hand, I read the handwritten slope on plain cardboard.

Tu étais où pendant tout ce temps?

"I know you've said you hate diamonds, so I thought this would be more meaningful."

When my eyes shoot up to look at him, he's on one knee. A simple gold band glints in his hand.

"You are clever, resilient, and incredible. I need you. More than that, I needed to show you that I will devote myself to protecting you and making you as happy as you make me. When that bomb went off, I couldn't locate you for several minutes. I was terrified. I thought you had died, and I'd never make it right between us, or hold you again. I know it's only been a few months, but I need you to know how much," his voice breaks, "you've always meant to me."

I press my palm against his cheek. "Even when... I'm insulting you?"

"*Especially* when." His eyes crinkle, but his voice still comes out raw. "I think of it as a bit of foreplay."

I throw back my head with a laugh, then my mind fills with the realization of what is happening. The box is so light in my hands, equal to the weight of the air in my lungs. My heart pounds, but I am not afraid. My cheeks become wet, and my eyes find his. He stares longingly at me, the adoration in his undeniable.

"Amara Rhodes, you have ruined me of anyone else. Will you do me the honor of spending your life with me?"

Since Warsaw, I've come to understand who Henry is: a man of integrity, who challenges me, makes me laugh, and—I would never admit it aloud—is patient when I push him to his limits. The things I'd misunderstood about him have become the very qualities I never want to live without. There is so much more to him, to us, now. We survived a bomb together, and in the aftermath of what happened, I was shown that my love for him is inexorable. It was only a matter of accepting it.

"I will," I say, pulling him up to kiss me. He stands, fingers beneath my chin. His lips are feathery soft, and when they press against my mouth, it feels as if anything is possible. Rain pours over the city, a storm permeating with change in the distance. We hold onto each other like one does to life when standing at the end of the world.

Chapter Twenty-Seven

We take a cab to city hall. Henry arranges for total discretion. We marry after hours with one employee and a confidential marriage license. Our hands clasp onto one another.

"I take you, Amara, as my wife, my partner, my equal." His eyes scan me. "I vow to protect you from harm, and love you as much as the first day, every day."

I try to memorize this moment. Resignation had convinced me to believe I would never have this. Standing at the threshold, my hands squeeze Henry's as I take a leap of faith.

"I take you, Henry, as my husband, my partner, my equal. I vow my love and my loyalty for all of my life. How—" my voice catches, "how glad I am to have been wrong that love would never find me. For every exquisite part of love that took its time, I'm so happy to say these words now by your side."

Chapter Twenty-Eight

London, England, Five days until France

Emerson gives us the news without preamble one night in the sitting room of his house.

"There were two prominent deaths last night: a parliamentary leader in Berlin named Abenwald was shot in his home... and Roman Górski."

"The head of Tatrialny?" I gasp. There is nothing that could have prepared me for this.

Henry and I look at Emerson in shock. My mind reels. Is this a surprise to Emerson? What would a man do if he were helping a criminal organization and the head of it died?

"How?" asks Henry, his voice hard.

"Abenwald's body was discovered in broad daylight in his car," says Emerson brusquely. "Górski was found dead outside his home next to his two bodyguards."

I have to play my part, because it's crucial that Emerson never suspects the work of our side op. So I pose my question as if walking along a tight rope, because it's more than just a question; the answer is a compass.

"Who stands to benefit with Górski gone?"

"We've yet to learn who the second-in-command will be," Emerson answers, slicing the air with his hand with purpose. "Though I suspect someone who has been in Tatrialny for a long time. A syndicate like that won't be left to someone new." He says it with such forcefulness, I realize I've only seen this side of him once before. It was years ago, when I'd gotten into an accident in a rental car after a weekend in Somerset. He'd been so upset when I said I was fine to work the next day, saying that if I went to the office, he would have Helen herself take me back home.

"Isn't Górski's death what we want?" I ask, looking between them. "If it really is the head of Tatrialny, isn't this good?"

"His death will have an immense ripple effect across the syndicate as a whole, and what changes will be made by this are unknown. Whereas before we knew who we were dealing with, now we're going to be blind," says Emerson.

"Who's next in line to inherit the trafficking network?" I ask.

"Górski was hard to surveil, hard to follow," states Henry. "The answer to that has been obscured by the network's stealth security and their tap into local law enforcement."

"What we need is more information. Specifically, everything that is on that device," says Emerson as he moves to stand. Setting down his glass on the coffee table, he looks across the room at Henry.

"Verify as many details as possible with your contact in Warsaw within the next 48 hours," he orders. "See what they have, what they know. Go in person and do it through the usual channels. We need to determine the cause of death and who might have done it."

A spike of panic impales into my chest at the thought of Henry back in Warsaw. He doesn't look at me, only pushes a shoulder off the wall and straightens.

"Yes, sir," he says with a serious nod. Beneath his calm mask, I detect the imperceptible trace of effect; his slow blink, the clenching of his jaw.

I swallow and ask, "Will the news report it?"

"Media reports will be vague on the cause of death, given it was an inside job," answers Henry. "Tatrialny has deep pockets and resources to control the narrative. Given the amount of protection that'd been on Górski, it is highly improbable this was an inside job."

"Whoever it is, they have something to gain," says Emerson. "And they're now a high-value target to anyone else who knows and brings that information to any competing groups. Bring me that device when you return. Given current events, we need to accelerate our efforts. Utilizing the agency's resources will increase our chances of preventing self-detonation."

My mind spins, a whirlpool of various possibilities. For months, we've successfully evaded giving Emerson the drive. Was this a ruse constructed by him, made to manipulate us into a sense of urgency that will give in to his demands for the device? I'm caught in a grip of unknowing and fear.

"Understood," says Henry without hesitation. "I'll book the next flight out."

Emerson gives a nod, and I begin to follow out the door when he stops me with a palm in the air. "Amara, mind if I have a minute?"

Henry's out in the hall and glances back at me. Where only I can see, he stays where he is. I give an imperceptible nod and grasp the knob to close the door.

"Everything okay?" I ask neutrally, trying to mask my unease. Since beginning to work covertly on the case, I've not spent much time alone with Emerson. Any sense of normal conversation dies in my throat at the fact that two more people have died related to this operation, and someone is responsible. Was it him?

"How long has that been going on?" He points to the door with a wry smile.

I only blink in surprise, unprepared for this question. I sense the immediate danger that Emerson knows. It's information he could pass along to the syndicate. This might be putting us at risk. But I also can't deny my marginal relief that he isn't trying to discuss anything related to the case.

"There have been a few fewer insults his way," he says. "You're also not as good at hiding your feelings as you think."

Teetering on the border of how best to approach this conversation, I quickly decide the only way to get through this conversation is as truthfully as possible. Emerson will expect to speak with me like we always have. I play along.

"I should have known niceness would be the giveaway," I say, biting back a smile. "Should've been more heavy-handed with the name-calling."

"I can't say I'm surprised," he says with a head shake and a laugh.

"He's a very good agent, and you're my favorite protégé."

"I don't think you're supposed to have favorites," I joke.

"I'm trying to say, I think he's a brilliant match for you. He's very discerning, and you are someone who needs a person not easily deterred by hardship. That is all any of us want out of love," he says, and from the way he says it, I know he's thinking of Helen. "We want it to transcend all the misfortune and grief life has to offer."

"I really thought I hated him. Surprised the hell out of me," I say, letting out a dramatic sigh.

"It's a thin line," says Emerson with a chuckle. I realize then how profoundly I've missed talking to him. The easy conversation is a spark of familiarity, so akin to my friendship with him over the years that it crushes inside my chest.

"The workplace isn't quite where I expected to meet someone," I say with a laugh.

He rests a hand on my shoulder. "I'm glad we recruited you. If it hadn't been for Tobias's recommendation, we might never have known what could have been."

"What's Tobias got to do with my working there?" I give him a puzzled look.

"Ah, well," says Emerson a bit sheepishly. "He was the one who recommended you, but asked if I could keep it private. He didn't want you to think you were getting preferential treatment in case the hiring process went smoothly."

"I didn't know that," I tell him with surprise. "You'd never said anything before."

"To be honest, I'd only been reminded of it recently," he says. I make a note to ask Tobias about it sometime next week at work when I see him. Emerson glances over my shoulder and notices the time.

"It's getting late, I should let you get home."

I give him a smile and nod before I navigate around a sofa chair. I'm counting the steps until I can leave, until I can cry into my hands, or shake Henry and say, *What if we're wrong? What if the only thing he's guilty of is saving us from a worse harm, and we don't know it?*

"Goodnight," I tell him, giving a wave.

"Goodnight, Amara."

Emerson, in the chair, appears contemplative as I head out. Words gather on the tip of my tongue, to call out or say something, but I stop myself. The ease of the conversation muddies everything for me: the past, the present, the future. *How could you?* I want to ask him. *Why have you betrayed not only your country but also me?*

***

Forty-eight hours pass as I clean my entire flat so thoroughly that boredom blends into worry. I read long-form tech articles on database structures and transistors. I'm restless, anxious. Picking up my phone every ten minutes or so, then setting it down. My chest fills with terror at what Henry might come back to say. Memories of us nearly being killed by the bomb regularly drum beneath my skin, like a ticking clock recounting backwards to the tragedy. I relive it in nightmares where I wake up in a cold sweat. I remind myself that Henry is more than capable and that if there is a man who can evade death solely to torture me, it will be him.

In the late afternoon of the third day, a rattle at my front door startles me. I mute the TV. Inching silently to the door, I reach for the baseball bat leaning against the entryway table. My disposable phone is charging on the table, and there are no missed calls or messages. There's a stampede behind my chest. Surely if it was Henry, he would have let me know, he would have—

Henry's face freezes when he sees the bat swinging toward him.

"Oy!"

"Why didn't you call me first, you idiot?" I scowl.

"That's how I know I'm in the right place," he says raggedly. Shutting the door behind him, he sets his backpack down on the floor.

Resting the bat against the wall, I wrap my arms around him. His fingers, warm and familiar, cradle against my back. His nose presses into my neck with a deep inhale.

"Amara—we need to talk."

I pull back to look at him. His dark lashes frame tired eyes, heavy with the weight of the past few days and all it has taken from him.

"What happened?" My fingers tighten. "What did Antoni say?"

He braces himself against the counter and looks at me.

"Antoni was killed."

Chapter Twenty-Nine

London, England, Two days until France

No, no, no.

"A car bomb," he adds grimly in the wake of my shock. With faint smudges under his eyes, he looks like he hasn't slept in days. "It happened right after the first dead letter drop. He risked his life to get me information."

I want to take hold of his arms and have him speak slower, tell him to spell it out for me. Antoni has been Henry's informant, but he was also our only hope of preventing worse disasters.

"Antoni passed along a name in the first dead letter box." I hear the tense undertow in his words. "Amara—we were wrong about Emerson. It isn't him."

My heart plummets. "You told me Antoni said someone had infiltrated MI6. Em—Emerson knew it was a signal device, that day in Warsaw. You didn't tell him that it had special coded technology. And he seemed to know other things, too. Wait—you said first. There was more than one?" I ask.

"There were two," he says, looking pained. "Antoni provided names."

I'm still reeling, my hand on the kitchen island as if I'm swaying along the deck of a boat. Antoni's death changes everything, but knowing Emerson didn't betray MI6 horrifies me almost more.

"What was the name?" I ask, looking up at him.

"Ostatni," he tells me. "I think it's a last name. I'll ask around, see who else might recognize it."

"Ostatni?" I ask. "That means last in Polish..." My attention snags on it, sounding familiar beyond the translation. Where have I heard that before? "You said there were two drops. What did you learn in the second one?"

"Someone named Sophie Vester is moving up the ranks in Tatrialny, and quickly," says Henry. "Vester isn't who killed Roman. Antoni knew there was a son, and he was killed for knowing it. But there is blood in the waters."

The ringing grows in sound at the second name that strikes me as familiar. *S. Vester.*

Suddenly, I'm reminded of where I'd seen it.

"Tobias. He—he received a call from someone by that name. I'd barely glanced at the screen, so it was only a second, but I saw it. We were in a pub." What would be the odds?

Then I gasp, remembering. I quickly reach for my phone. Henry stands in my periphery, coming closer. My fingers scroll on my phone. Scanning old emails, I scroll through them rapidly. I know exactly what I'm looking for. A moment later, and—yes. There. I turn it to show Henry.

"Do you see that?" I point just below the name on my screen.

"Ostatni foundation. That is a letter from them granting me a full scholarship at Oxford."

He's shaking his head. "And you're saying..."

"Tobias is involved," I say breathlessly. "Somehow in all of this. Emerson told me the other night that Tobias recommended me for MI6, that's how I was recruited. Emerson mentioned Tobias had wanted to keep it private. But why? I didn't meet Tobias until my first year of service."

Henry looks from my phone to my face a few times. A sharp expression pinches between his brows.

"I never realized until now—you have the same smile."

"As who?"

"As Tobias," he says with disquiet. "I always thought he's been focused on you for some reason. It only just occurred to me. *He* might be Ostatni. When Antoni said someone had infiltrated MI6, he must have meant *him*."

Had he really been hiding in plain sight? With blinding clarity, I realize what has been right in front of me this entire time; Tobias's interest in me and the way it never felt romantic. The vague mention of his half-sister. A touch of envy I could never quite figure out. *I* am the half-sister. And if my mother died, but Tobias's father is my own, that means...

Nothing makes sense.

"We need to talk to Emerson," I say, the words rushing out like wind through a tunnel. Throwing on a pair of shoes, I hurry to grab a coat.

When we run out the door, my heart is beating rapidly. Thoughts rush over the other like water over a rock. My mind races to comprehend that we were wrong about Emerson. The truth was staring me in the face the entire time, and I was too slow to see it.

What have we done?

CHAPTER THIRTY

LONDON, ENGLAND, FIFTEEN HOURS UNTIL FRANCE

Whatever calm I'd felt before Henry had returned was well and gone now. Weaving around pedestrians and street debris, down isolated alleys, we race to Emerson's. Every few moments, I check over my shoulder. When it feels like someone is watching us, it's nothing but my own shadow. Worse, because reality is far more unsettling than my imagination this time.

The streets of London are quiet as we sneak past the familiar long row of hedges. Without cloud cover, the inky night hovers around us, obscuring details near his back gate. When we notice the back door ajar, blood rushes to my head.

"Something's wrong," I say in a hushed voice.

His palm quietly pushes the edge of the door further. It opens without a sound, and we advance through the dark of the kitchen. I don't trust the silence. I remember that Helen is out of town, that it's only Emerson.

A *thump* rattles the ceiling above us, like a body thrown against a wall. A floorboard creaks in a different spot, a violent sound to my ears when I realize Emerson is not here alone.

My mind begins to rattle in its cage as worry blooms in my chest. Another rattle, this time the unmistakable sound of a body hitting a wall. Henry and I carefully begin to ascend the stairs. A slant of light from a room cuts across the floor like the blade of a knife. Furniture scatters outside of it, broken into pieces. There are voices, indistinct at first through the wall, though they become clearer as we reach the top step. My feet follow behind Henry's, step for step. To our right is an empty room, and we conceal ourselves in the shape of shadows.

"The other knee this time," a first voice says. I recognize the register, oiliness replacing all politeness.

A savage noise comes from the room, and I realize it's Emerson crying out in pain. My hands are shaking as it dawns on me how much, and that its threat of fatality is the entire point. My eyes adjust to the dark, and I can see Henry's eyes on the door. Another set of footsteps indicates Tobias isn't alone. He didn't even have the guts to do the dirty work himself.

"Save yourself the trouble and tell me where you hid the device," says Tobias.

"You can't trust the information that led you here," says Emerson. "Nothing you've been told can be trusted, which is exactly what needed to happen."

"Trying to convince me I can't trust anyone is a waste of your breath," says Tobias. "Where is it? Who are you protecting? Is it her?"

I look at Henry, my heart skipping a beat.

Emerson gives a laugh cut sharply by a cough. "It was only me. I knew someone in MI6 was feeding information to Tatrialny, I just didn't know it was you betraying your country."

I can hear the sneer from the other room. "I wouldn't wish being British on my worst enemy. And you must think I'm some kind of idiot if I'm to believe you don't have a failsafe."

I picture Emerson stubbornly staying silent. Why bother arguing with someone when you know they're going to kill you anyway?

"You're mistaken if you think you'll get another chance," says Tobias, as if they're chatting about the season, or a holiday. "You are the only one who can end your suffering."

Emerson speaks through a wheezing breath. "Kill me, or don't, any information you want will have to die with me—"

Before he can finish, there's a muffling shot from a silencer. A body collapses. The immediate quiet following it is an arrow splintering directly into my chest, like a hatchet lodging itself into my ribcage, aiming for my heart but stealing my breath instead. Without thought, my foot takes a half-step toward the light in the hall. Henry seizes my wrist. *No*, his shaking head tells me. Eyes brimming, I look in the direction of where I know Emerson is dead. We don't have a gun, we don't have a way to outmaneuver. Tobias and his lackey, with their gun, outnumber us. Danger is a breath away as I retreat into shadows. I am cloaked in my own cowardice.

"Useless," says Tobias with a sigh. "Bring the vehicle around, I'll be down in a moment."

My gaze darts back to the voice of Tobias around the corner. He switched to speaking in perfect Polish. Heavy footsteps stomp down the stairs and out the door. I grip Henry's arm in the dark. This might be our only chance to get Tobias while he's alone, but when Tobias starts speaking again, I freeze.

"I know you were protecting her somehow." His voice is low, absent of the cruelty he'd had only minutes before. I strain to hear. "If I have no remorse over killing my own father, a sister with only half my blood is no thought at all. But it must be done. And it's a good thing I dug up her address, yeah? A shame you won't be there to hear her scream."

At the sound of his walking out of the room, we hold our breath. In the crack of the door, I see him holding his phone with gloves on. Its screen illuminates his face as he heads down the stairs. A moment later, I hear a car door shut in the distance outside. Only when we're certain they're gone do I heave gasping breaths. Henry slowly walks toward the room.

Walking behind him, Emerson comes into view. He's slumped with his back against the bed frame. Blood pools, and a trail of it begins to travel at an angle away from his body. My heart hammers in my chest to see it by the light of a lone lamp. I back up slowly, my arm brushing against the open door.

"Don't touch anything," he orders. "You've blood on you."

Instantly raising my arm away from the door, I see a length of blood across the back of my sleeve. It's a dark shade of burgundy. It almost looks like a handprint on my clothes that shouts for attention, saying, *Don't look away, this is all that's left of him.* I become lightheaded.

"Emerson must have known Tobias was connected to Tatrialny somehow," says Henry. "He might have speculated if it was one or both of you infiltrating MI6, but Tobias showing up for the signal device tonight and demanding to know if Emerson was protecting you all but confirmed it."

In a daze, my breath feels short, but I try to focus on what he's saying. There's so much blood.

"Amara, did you understand what he said?" asks Henry, a deepening groove of worry appearing. "He was speaking Polish, right?"

"Yes. He said—he said..." My eyes shift back to Emerson's limp body, growing cold.

"I know this is really difficult, but I need you to tell me what he said." The sound of my name from Henry's mouth cleanses Tobias's mention of me in his.

I try to think. "He thinks Emerson was protecting me. Somehow, he knew I was involved in the case. He admitted to killing his father. That he was going to—" I come out of shock as I begin to translate. "Henry, he has my address. He's going to try to kill me."

Henry walks toward me and, without touching the tainted sleeve, pulls me hurriedly down the stairs.

I look behind us in confusion. "We can't leave him like that. He—Emerson didn't do anything wrong."

"We know that now," he says gently. We reach the bottom landing, and he continues to pull me to the back garden door. He takes my face with both hands and forces me to look at him.

"You need to leave for the safe house," he says, half-statement, half-plea.

I recoil. "What? No."

"Tobias knew Emerson had information on the hard drive, and he's coming for you. Not only is he dangerous, but we know what kind of power he has. I don't know how he became an agent, or how he knew you were part of this, but right now we know who Tobias is within Tatrialny, and he didn't mention me to Emerson. Which means this is my only chance to get ahead of him. I'm going to remove traces of us here, and we can't waste time."

"But it wasn't supposed to be like this," I cry. "Emerson wasn't supposed to—"

"I know, love," he says, leaning into me. "We talked about this. When the time came, it would have to happen quickly. Do you remember what I said?"

I meet his gaze, holding my breath. His eyes fill with devotion, with fear.

"If I don't go now, then it will all have been for nothing," I recite tearfully. I cry harder. The night has become a maelstrom of all my worst fears made real. Here, I would not be abandoned, but I would be the one to abandon. I had to. For Emerson. For the children who had already died. For the ones we still needed to protect. Everything else was unknown.

Giving a nod of relief that I understand, Henry drops his hands.

"Do you remember the instructions I gave you? How to get there?"

"Yes." My lip quivers, tasting salt.

His lips press against mine briefly. There isn't time to linger. There is no erasing, only enduring, now.

"I can never go back to a time before you, remember that," he says. Abruptly opening the back door, he urges me out. "*Run*, and don't look back."

My final image of him is the way his eyes darken, the way the distance between us grows. The world shifts and disappears beneath my feet. I run anyway, leaving him behind.

CHAPTER THIRTY-ONE

THIRTEEN HOURS UNTIL FRANCE

I run two slippery miles to my destination, checking behind me at every turn to make sure I'm not being followed. After shutting off my phone for tracking purposes, I power it back on briefly. Because Henry and I had left for Emerson's with only the bare essentials, I only have my personal phone with me. The disposable phone sits on a shelf in my kitchen. I have almost nothing in my possession.

At a trash bin, I breathe heavily from running in the damp and cold. I quickly type out a message to James.

James—

Can't make happy hour drinks. It's as I suspected, I'm far more important than you. Make sure to have a lavender Pastis without me.

Amara

As soon as it sends, I tear out the battery and toss it. At the next few bins across several blocks, I remove the SIM card, then shed the remnants of anything else that could trace my whereabouts. I might never be able to go to my flat again.

When I arrive at a storage locker facility, I enter the code Henry has keyed in for access. Our wedding date. The locker beeps, giving a brief flash of green. Grabbing the leather duffels, I shut the locker and check my surroundings before opening them.

It was all there as he said it would be: passports with three different identities, a set of clothes, a folded paper map, keys for a car lot down the block, some kind of blade, and most crucially, the device. I pull it out, remove the jacket, and tuck my hair beneath a cap. From the second duffel, I pick the first passport I see: Nora Carter. Placing it in my jacket pocket for easy access, I zip everything shut. Hurrying, I lift the hood of the jacket over my head to shield myself and head out.

London is a slow drizzle of my sorrow, with fear clinging to me as visibly as the air out of my lungs. I make my way to the car park, and when I find the small, two-door vehicle at the end of the lot on the 14th row, I check my surroundings one last time. Clicking the unlock button, it chirps twice in response. I place both duffels in the passenger seat and hurry to start the car. With a quick check in the glove compartment, I'm satisfied to find four spare license plates. Rain slants across the windshield as I drive toward the Eurotunnel to leave England.

I follow the winding roads and reflective signs that lead me toward the terminals in Folkestone and Calais. I eye every camera as I drive through. I know later, if someone looks for it, there will be footage showing this car boarding a carriage of the shuttle, giving me away. I pull the cap over my face a bit more. The line of cars ahead begins to slow on the deck of the shuttle. There's a pang in my chest to imagine Henry planning all of this when he knew he wouldn't be with me. My knuckles go white from gripping the steering wheel as we descend 75 meters below sea level. I feel I've hardly taken a full breath again until I exit the carriage and catch sight of the stars.

***

The weather in France, unlike London, is clear, though it still carries the chill of autumn. It's a long drive, but I don't stop until I have to. The fuel indicator's red blinks force my hand. I stop, mostly because there aren't many petrol stations available, especially in this part of France.

Dawn is still hours away, so I use my card at an unoccupied station. I feel a twinge in my shoulder from driving all night. While I'm filling up, a car drives slowly past. It's too dark, and the driver is too far for me to make out any details, but I swear they were watching me. Heart palpitations are uneven in my chest, and I hurry to remove the nozzle. I rush back into the car and keep driving. Every few seconds, I look in the rearview mirror to check that no one is following me, but in the dark, everything is a threat. Adrenaline keeps me wide-eyed and awake. I need to keep driving. I have to get to the safe house.

According to the markings on the map, I'm not far. Only my headlights illuminate the short distance in front of my car, and it's barely enough. There—a small cottage near a rural field. Pulling into the gravel drive, my head swivels every direction to check my surroundings. I had traveled on foot in London, made it through the Eurotunnel by car, and driven ten hours through France. This step feels like the hardest because it is the last one. After this, another kind of journey will begin: getting the device into safe hands.

The wrought iron gate is visible from the car. I close the car door quietly behind me.

In less than an hour, the sun will rise over the forgotten cottage, and it will be the first day of a hard journey ahead. Taking a lungful of air, I let it out, like a fog in the shape of the moon.

Henry had gotten me this far. The rest I would have to do on my own.

Chapter Thirty-Two

South of France, Present Day

"My darling," Henry breathes.

Puffs of exhale drift into the crook of my neck. My arm links around him and holds him tightly. Every atom craves to be closer, so I press against him, afraid I'll never be close enough.

"I didn't know what would happen." My voice is hoarse from crying. "I didn't know if I would ever see you again."

We're on the floor of the kitchen, rooted to the spot where I'd found him. After I calm down, he rises to stand and pulls me up gently with both hands. He wipes the last of my tears, his slender fingers across my cheeks.

"Did you know there's a chicken around here?" asks Henry. His eyes scan the room, and he cranes his neck to peer down the adjoining hallway.

"I believe you mean a chicken freeloads here, and I pay the bills."

"What?"

"Céline," I explain with a sigh.

"...Who is Céline?"

"The chicken you were just talking about," I say. "Obviously."

Henry's attention lasers toward a scratching sound at the door. He moves fast, pushing me behind him, and grabs the gun from the counter.

"It's all right, it's just Esse," I tell him, my hand on top of his to lower the gun.

"Esse is another chicken?" he asks, trying to keep up.

I give him a puzzling look. "Why would I keep one chicken inside but leave the other one out?"

"I dunno, I've never heard of anyone keeping a chicken in a house before," he says, throwing his hands in the air.

I press a kiss against his cheek. Pulling back, I go to open the door for Esse, who is throwing a tantrum from being left outside, mewling louder than I've ever heard her before. When I lean down to pick her up, she leaps further and faster than my hands can catch her. Without hesitation, she approaches Henry. He lowers to the ground and hands out his open palm. Esse purrs against it.

"As you can see, she lacks any self-preservation skills," I tell him wryly.

Her tail swishes back and forth behind her. Then, completely satisfied by the amount of affection she's acquired, Esse leaves us to curl up in her bed with a sleeping Céline, who barely rustles at the intrusion.

"Mystery solved," I say, pointing. "A future tip: if you ever can't find either of them, they're usually there."

Henry stands, something tender glittering in his eyes. I had missed seeing him with a ghost of a smile on that perfect mouth of his.

"You named her Esse. Like the poem?"

I give a nod, and he leans toward me, pulling me closer by the hand.

"Any other animals I should know about?" he asks.

"Well," I say, contemplative, "there's Albert, a Mérens colt. Don't be alarmed if you hear him tapping at the kitchen window. Céline sometimes tolerates him, but Esse will scratch at the door incessantly until she's let out to say hello. I think she believes she's the same size as him, but he doesn't seem to mind despite the racket she makes. It's very annoying."

He tilts his head.

"You're different here."

I lean against the kitchen counter, suddenly feeling shy.

"I..." My eyes adjust to the sight of him in the cottage, the way the room seems to breathe around his form. "The first few months were really, really hard. Living in London, I always believed I enjoyed—no, preferred—to be alone. Turns out, I actually *hate* being alone, especially as a forced choice. It wasn't only about missing you; it was about feeling like I had started out in this life alone, and I didn't want the remainder of my life to be the same way. Then, as some kind of cosmic joke, I couldn't get rid of these little beggars," I say, gesturing to the corner. "I didn't understand where they were coming from, or why they kept coming to *me*. But suddenly having them here made life bearable in a way I hadn't thought I'd want. They keep me company. These animals foisted themselves upon me, and not only can I not get rid of them, but now I don't want to.

I fixed the greenhouse, and this house, and planted flowers. I was trying to survive, but... I gave myself something more than that. I think I gave myself a home."

He studies me with a solemnity that breaks my heart. "I am grateful for them. I don't care how much you change, or whether you're the same person I met in London. I would love you still. I promised myself to you for the whole of my life. What you did to survive was not a matter of luck, but fortitude." His hands grasp mine, his skin warm in my palms. "I am so sorry you've been alone all these months. You'll never have to be alone like this again. Ever."

Without warning, my eyes blur my vision again. I am a leaking faucet now that Henry is here. I'd become so accustomed to the hollow and empty space in my heart without Henry that to have him with me now made me so heady it felt dreamlike. My body, having been constantly in a state of alert and anticipation, begins to melt from exertion and stress. A wave of fatigue takes over, and I'm suddenly very tired.

"Come, let's go to bed and get some rest," he says softly. "We can talk more tomorrow."

Turning off the lights and securing the door, we make our way to the back of the cottage. In bed, we lie in the shape of half-moon shells as our eyes greedily take in each other. His fingers trace the scar on my temple with a slow and gentle touch. My scar is a memory of so many things: terrible death, and a cacophony of what awaited us when the dust settled that day in Warsaw. The healing of that wound over time also catalogues an astonishing element of love that I can no longer imagine living without. I'm afraid to blink, to find that he's not really here, that I have indeed made him up. Henry must sense this because he presses his lips against each cheek, kissing me tenderly, heartache unspooling from him. Despite my exhaustion, we each stay awake for a long while. Long enough to witness the heavy weight of night melt into dawn, and we finally fall asleep.

***

I don't know how long I sleep, but I wake to daylight, the landscape bathed in a golden hue of sunset. Esse, the scoundrel, has made her way to my pillow and is curling around my head in her sleep. A clattering in the kitchen startles me until I remember Henry is here. I smell food from the kitchen and hear the familiar sound of the oven door closing. Slipping on a robe, I pad down the hallway with Esse following close behind. A radio is on low by the sink, and light filters in across Henry's broad shoulders. He hasn't seen me yet, and I lean against the far wall of the kitchen.

"Finally putting those hands to good use, I see."

He lets out a laugh before turning. "Would you like some coffee?"

I glance out the window. "Probably not, given the hour, otherwise I'll never be able to sleep tonight." I walk to him, wrapping my hands around his waist. "Are you really here? You're not actually a figment of my imagination, are you?"

"I had something of the same thought when you were pointing a gun at me." He gives me a kiss on the top of my head, then returns to whatever's sizzling on the stove.

"Smells good."

"You didn't have many provisions, so I used the last of the salmon and asparagus for dinner," he says, flipping over the fish in the pan. He sets the heat on low and turns back to me. Folding his hands at his back, he walks toward me in a predatory gait until I'm backed up against the wall. We're a breath apart, and his is warm on my neck, making my stomach curl.

"A dangerous pursuit," I whisper.

"So long as you're involved, I'm willing to take the risk," he replies in a low, husky voice. My lips meet his in a slow embrace, a dance that grows familiar with each passing moment. I want to linger in the space forever as we slowly make our way back to each other after so much time apart.

I pull back, sniffing smoke in the air. "I think the vegetables are burning."

"Shit." He quickly moves to shut off the oven and take out the asparagus. I watch him as I suppress a laugh. After we finish eating at the table, I set down my fork.

"I like the touch of thyme," I say.

He gestures to the window over the sink. "I stole it from the greenhouse. Pretty impressive what you've done, by the way."

I take his hand. "Why don't we go see it together? I need to take Céline out, anyway."

He smiles. "Show me everything. I want to see it all."

Céline and Esse follow behind in tandem down the slope of the hill. Henry stops to take in the bucolic view at dusk, the countryside of France in every inhale. A wave of calm washes over me as I do the same. Even after all this time here, it always feels like I'm seeing it for the first time—the vines taking over the glasshouse, the meadow, the copse of trees in the surrounding land. Light spilling over the top. Tranquility flowing into a life I had never asked for, but is something I now don't want to leave.

"It's strange to know this was the view my mother grew up with," he says, breaking the quiet. "It probably hasn't changed much."

In the greenhouse, warm, fragrant air envelops us. Only Esse joins us inside as I show Henry every plant and bloom that has sprung up in the last few weeks. I talk for a while about roses and radishes, and the use of ladybugs to take care of aphids. As I point here and there, I move a few things out of the way, including a small butane torch I'd used to solder one of the bent corners of the metal greenhouse frame. Henry listens patiently, navigating around a few scattering baskets full of garden tools and gloves I'd bought at local *brocantes.*

"Does it make you miss London?" he asks while his fingers graze a few leaves of lettuce. Esse pounces at the stalky leaf in a row of planted carrots.

"I don't. This country surely has its quirks with things closed on Sundays and the fact that I can't always communicate with other people," I muse. "But I love the history here. It makes me feel insignificant in the best way, because it means it's been here before me and will survive long after I'm gone. It's a practice in humility, honestly. A reminder that if nothing I do really matters, then I get to choose what matters to me. This place matters to me," I say, my hands sweeping the air. "After we get the device to a secure place, I think I want to stay here. Don't worry—it's in a safe deposit box in a town a half hour away."

He gives me a smile, but it's tense. Forgetting everything else, I finally ask him what has been on my mind since I arrived in France.

"Are you going to tell me what happened to Tobias?" I ask. "Did you find me to bring me back to London?"

His jaw clenches, and he looks reluctant all of a sudden.

"I—no. It's better that you stay here."

I watch him, trying to relearn him, his tells. A thought occurs to me.

"I'm such an idiot not to have thought of it sooner." My heart hammers in panic. "Does the service suspect me of killing Emerson because I disappeared?"

His hand lowers at his side. "No. That night you left for the safe house, I ensured you had a cover. I hacked into his email that night and crafted correspondence between you two going back a few months, where you said you might return to America for personal reasons. There was a one-way ticket purchased with your card to San Francisco with a timestamp departure hours before Emerson's body was found. I placed your belongings in a storage facility and rented out your flat. Tobias seems to have had no idea we were involved. Almost eerily normal at headquarters. He's the same prick he's always been."

He'd thought of everything. Henry had forced me to leave so I would be safe, and then did everything in his power in London to ensure it. Yet, as my eyes survey the searing expression on his face, there's a bracing look that tells me there's something more.

"What is it then?" I straighten, tense. "What aren't you saying?"

"The week after Emerson was killed, the foreign minister appointed another chief."

"Of course," I say, chewing on my lip as I think. "It wouldn't be Tobias... It could be someone familiar enough with Vauxhall Cross, or perhaps someone newer to the agency whose visibility would be accepted by the media. Someone outside of MI6?"

"And that someone would have an interest in obtaining immediate, unfettered access to high-level security information," he says. "Someone who could keep an eye and ear on everything."

"*No.*" My breath walks along a tightrope, gripped by a sudden thought. Why hadn't I seen it before? Who else close to Tatrialny might stand to gain control over the most powerful security services in the world?

"Yes," he says with a solemn nod. "Sophie Vester is now the chief of the Secret Intelligence Office."

Chapter Thirty-Three

In the warm, humid air of the greenhouse, Henry tells me everything. I turn over a large bucket and sit. He tells me about watching Tobias's movements and that he had asked around for me after I'd left. A lot of attention was fixated on Emerson's murder, splashing the pages of newspapers and grabbing the attention of a famous director, who is now working on a documentary series about Emerson's life and death. When he mentions the device, my heart sinks in my chest. I stand to put my hands on his arms.

"The technical obstacle of it is still the same. It's not a matter of encryption, and taking the risk of bringing it to someone with advanced technology who can access it was not one I was willing to take. But I've been researching, and I think I'm close to a solution."

He runs a hand over his face.

"I know, Henry. I've been trying," I say helplessly.

"I suppose I'd hoped..."

"You'd hoped I'd found a way to solve all our problems and get the information we need?" I reply. My hands grip the frame of a cedar plant bed of tomatoes. "No, unfortunately, with these rudimentary conditions and without field expertise as an agent, I'm not very helpful here. Pretty much useless, in fact."

"That's not what I'm saying—"

The words rush out. "Don't you think I'm trying? Do you think I wanted to leave you and my entire life in London behind?"

"I was without you, too, Amara." His jaw clenches. "I had to find a way to live without you so I could carry on with the investigation by myself."

"I didn't ask for you to do that. I could have stayed. I could have helped."

"I needed you to be safe," he says with a shake of his head. "If you had stayed, Tobias would have found you and killed you just like he did Emerson. I told you before, I am not willing to risk your life—"

"Mine is not the only one to save!" I say in a thunderous shout, whirling on him. My feet knock over the bucket, scaring Esse. "I didn't just leave for me! I did not want to be responsible for Tobias getting his hands on the drive or allowing him to use children as pawns in Tatrialny's schemes. I want that information more than anything else. I got here and grew some fucking *vegetables*. I took in some animals. It's not enough—it's shameful."

I refuse to cry, tears burning the edges of my eyes. He's silent, but approaches me tentatively. Only when his hands brush along my arms do I cover my face with my hands. My shoulders tremble as I sob, every minute standing in for each time I'd been afraid Tobias knew Henry was my husband and would find a way to kill him. He was here in front of me, and still, I could not shed the months of terror of not knowing what was going on beyond this tiny town in a country where no one knew me.

"Being safe here isn't shameful, but you're not the only one who feels guilty," he whispers. I look up at him through tear-filled lashes. "If I'm honest, I did want to protect the device, but I wanted to protect you more. I waited my entire life for you, and it killed me to watch you leave that night. But staying behind meant I could watch Tobias and gather evidence. If I thought for one moment he might go after you, I would have fucking killed him."

"It's horrible, too," I say in the quiet of the greenhouse with a slow shudder. "To know that not only did he kill Emerson and his own father, but that I'm connected to him by blood. It feels far worse than thinking I'm alone in this world to know that I'm related to a monster."

Chapter Thirty-Four

"Humphrey."

"No."

"Hobart."

"You sound like someone's uncle removed from a family tree."

"Don't insult my mother's favorite brother," he says with false sternness.

I give a scoff. "I highly doubt it, given how atrocious it would be for French people to pronounce."

I'm packing a late-afternoon picnic basket as we discuss an alias for him, though he's as difficult as I remember him being, and it warms me to know it.

"What's with the goofy smile?" he asks.

"Nothing," I say, then change the subject so he won't pester me more about it. "Are you ready to go?"

He takes the basket from my hands, full of two dozen oysters I'd picked up earlier from the fish market, and lemons. I carry a bottle of white wine and follow him out the door. We trek down the slope and further beyond the greenhouse, where a pond rests beneath a wooden pier. Camellias and magnolias bloom along the edges of the water. Chirping birds echo from the surrounding trees. Light shimmers off the surface in small ripples from a breeze. Gray cranes swim majestically along the surface.

The air is warm, and the afternoon sun shines behind an opaque cloud. We sit across a blanket I'd brought and hang our feet off the pier. Henry sits beside me with the basket between us. Being here with him is a joy, unlocking in my chest where only he holds the key. Reaching for two oyster knives, I hand him one, and we begin to shuck and eat. My hands smell like the brine of oysters. The day is so soft I nearly forget about the war we're fighting.

"Could never have this in London," he comments, watching birds chase one another mid-air.

Uncorking the bottle of wine, I make a small pour into an empty shell of oyster.

"Brilliant," he said, extending his own empty shell. After drinking from it, he tosses it into the paper bag we brought. "I meant to tell you. I spoke with James."

I pause, lowering the oyster I'd had halfway to my mouth.

"Is that so?"

"You could have told me James was a woman."

I give a shrug, but the derisive curl of my lips gives me away. "What would've been the fun in that?"

He throws his head back with a deep laugh. My favorite sound in the entire world.

"Is she okay?" I ask. I'd worried most about James, hoping she wasn't too distraught about my disappearance.

"She was fairly frantic after a vague message you'd sent her. She'd figured out that you were in the South of France, but suspected something had happened and found a secure way to contact me to find out if you were okay. I told her enough to reassure her you were safe," he says reassuringly. "I'm curious though, what did you tell her?"

"About us?"

"About the investigation. Or both, I suppose."

I hesitate. "She's the only family I've ever had. She's always known who you are. We left the orphanage in Warsaw within a year of each other—her to London, while I moved across the Atlantic," I explain. "She's why I moved to London after my adoptive parents passed away. Technically, I didn't tell her anything explicitly about the investigation."

When his brows shoot up, I place a hand on his arm.

"I need you to hear me when I say I trust James with my life. The fact that you're the only person who has found me tells me everything I need to know. She would rather be tortured than let anything happen to me."

"I do trust you, love," he says softly. "You were the only person in the world I could have trusted with the device. I placed the burden of the world in your hands, and you kept it safe."

I let out an exhale, my eyes shuttering close as the soft white of his knuckles graze my cheek. When I open them, he's holding out something in the palm of his hand.

A wedding ring, made up of a half-dozen pearls nestling on a delicate gold band. It steals my breath to see it.

"I knew I wanted to marry you the first time you insulted me," he tells me with a soft grin that fades into something painfully adoring. "This is the only life we get, and I want to spend it all with you."

He places the ring on my finger, then raises it to his lips. I'd missed it earlier, but as he does, I see a matching gold band sans pearls on his own finger. The sun slowly dips toward the horizon in the distance. I kiss him deeply, feeling pliant. We push aside the basket, the oysters, the wine. His hand travels from my feet to my legs, until it's lightly grazing my stomach under the dress I'm wearing. He lifts it until it's nearly off, watching me while he removes the thin fabric of my panties. Sliding it off each ankle, he brings his mouth against mine. The kiss is soft, full of tender heartache. It deepens between us until we are only skin and air and tongue and teeth. The pastoral world around us blurs with insignificance. At this moment, the world is sympathetic, soft, pleasing. His fingertips run down the length of my naked ribcage, and I curve my hips to meet his seeking hand.

"You are madness and delight, and I love you with every part of me," he whispers into the shell of my ear. He smells of fresh air and soap. "I'll never let anything bad happen to you."

I tremble in the half-dark of dusk, relinquishing my moans into the summer gloam. I let him spread my legs further apart as I yield to the demands of his fingers, his low voice in the crook of my neck. He slides in, the heel of his hand wringing out every ounce of tension in my body. Pleasure burns inside me, drawing out a pleading groan against his mouth as he hurtles me toward a crescendo, a sacred place deep inside me. My hands grip his shoulders, my own fingers digging into his skin. The solid weight of him is a heady power to have within reach. I am so close to a peak he's building me toward with his fingers. It climbs and climbs, until the freefall of ecstasy has me gasping out. At the unbearable, inescapable crest, his eyes are as black as the moon dipping in ink. He holds me close as my body releases shudder after shudder. He catches the cries from my mouth like they are something to eat.

The sky is a torch in the final moments of daylight. Panting, my breaths start to slow until they return to normal. With him, the world is both lovely and ravishing. After a few moments, he withdraws his hand to lower my dress over my hips and lie beside me. Bending his elbow, he leans against his palm and gives me a look that is both possessive and adoring.

I give him a sly look.

"You're looking at me as if we hadn't already gotten married, you would do it again."

He gently slings an arm over my waist and brings me into him.

"I would, and I will," he says, his velvet voice a cocoon. "I will ask you every day of my life if I have to, to know that you'll always say yes."

Chapter Thirty-Five

Esse sits at Henry's feet when I walk into the living room, swishing her tail clean across the floor. From the direction and heat of the midday sun, the day appears warm already. Henry's in the chair, reading an article on my laptop about advanced devices and their computing processes.

"There's something I want to talk to you about," I say, and Henry looks up from the article. "But I need you to stay open-minded."

"Is it a weird sex thing?"

I snort with derisiveness.

"It *is* a weird sex thing," he says with a flash of a grin. "It's okay, I know all about your handcuff fetish."

"*No*, it's a spy thing." I throw a dish towel at him.

He sets the laptop aside, and I pull up a dining chair to face him.

"We keep talking about how we are running out of time to get the information on the device, but we have a solution staring us in the face. We have James," I say, watching his face carefully. "We know the stakes; they're stacked high against us. I trust her to help us not only access it without it self-destructing but also get it into safe hands at

MI5. I know you're going to say it's a major risk, but it's all a risk. Even this, even now. It's a risk to keep sitting on the information we have. Tatrialny isn't only a foreign threat, but a national one to Great Britain. They'll have the jurisdiction, the justification, and the resources. This is our chance to get every scrap of evidence to put a lot of bad people away for a long time."

"I agree," he says. "I think we should."

The argument I'd prepared myself for deflates in my lungs. "Really?"

"Yes. In order to stop Tobias and, moreover, Tatrialny's grip on governments all over Western and Eastern Europe, we have to take a risk to get the intel. We need every name, every bit of proof we can get our hands on. If you trust James, I trust that."

"So we'll go back to London, talk to James, and make sure it goes to the head of MI5?" I ask.

"A nearly perfect plan," he says nonchalantly. "So long as you stay here."

This fucking man. "Absolutely not."

"Amara—"

"You're out of your goddamn mind if you think I'm going to stay behind *again* and let you deal with everyone on your own," I tell him firmly. "This is the non-negotiable part of the plan. It will be better if I'm there to assure James of what she's helping with. She doesn't know you yet. She isn't going to do your bidding simply on hearsay. This is a big ask if we need her to use MI5 resources to access the device. She'll need to hear it from me."

It's a stubborn standoff between us. He's leaning forward with his elbows on his knees while daggers shoot out of my eyes.

"Fine," he relents flatly. "But we stay together the entire time. If Tobias catches wind that you're in London, it's going to throw chaos into everything. We go to London, give it to James, and explain everything to the head of MI5. It will probably be escalated to the foreign secretary and head of domestic security, given the urgency." He frowns, leaning back in his chair with a sigh and a menacing look. "This might actually work."

Satisfied, I lean forward to kiss him.

"Now, was that so hard?"

***

An hour later, we're packing up. Clothes are in disarray as I grab items to place inside a duffel. Henry's gathering some of his belongings. He comes into the bedroom after I hang up from a call with Delphine, asking her to watch after Céline and Esse.

"She said it wasn't a problem," I tell him. "I told her it'll be a few weeks, but she didn't mind."

"I know it'll be tough to leave the cat behind, but we'll be back," he says with a kiss on my forehead.

Anxiety twists in my stomach, but I play it off. "She won't even miss me; she only goes where the food is."

"Hmm," he says with a knowing smile. "Speaking of which—why

don't you finish packing here, and I'll go into town to grab some provisions? It'll be a long drive back to Coquelles, so we can take the tunnel. Especially since we'll need to stop by and pick up the device from the deposit box."

I push back my hair. "That'd be great. I'll try to be quick so we can get on the road before dark."

"Any requests?" he asks as he begins to walk out of the room.

"Chocolates, something salty, and maybe a few croissants?"

"Got it. I'll be back in less than an hour," he calls out behind him. I hear the front door close and catch Esse trying to crawl into the duffel bag.

"I'm so sorry," I say with a sincerity that surprises me. My hands scratch behind her ears. "I'll come back, though. And I'll give you all the treats you'd ever want, I promise."

She hops off the bed and heads down the hall. I can hear Céline *tuk-tuk-tuk* from the front room. I finish packing and set the bag next to the door. I wander from room to room, eventually stopping in front of the window over the sink that frames the greenhouse. Esse wends herself around my legs.

"Come on, let's go for a visit to water the plants," I say. She follows after me out the door while Céline gives us a side eye and settles even deeper into her bed. Putting on a pair of wellies, I head down the slope toward the glasshouse. Esse scampers in, and I close the door behind us. Grabbing a shovel from a basket and the water canister, I begin to fill it in the sink.

"What should we water first? Food or flowers?" I say to Esse as she walks elegantly along a thin strip of a planter box. She runs toward the back of the greenhouse, all cares forgotten at the sight of a small rodent.

As I water the first row of tomatoes, I hear the door shut softly behind me.

"If you forgot the chocolate, it's probably grounds for divorce," I call out to Henry.

A chilling voice replies.

"I've been looking everywhere for you."

Chapter Thirty-Six

At the sound of Tobias's voice, my heart pitches over a cliff of fear. I'd been standing on the precipice for days, weeks, months. Slowly, I turn.

He watches me from the opposite end of the greenhouse with a gun pointing my direction, blocking the only way out. It's spine-chilling to see him. There's a hard look on his face, and even from a distance, his eyes look empty, unfeeling. His trench coat and leather boots appear out of place against the green and rustic background of the greenhouse. A gold watch flashes at his wrist. Both his attire and the expression he wears are startling; it's as if I'm witnessing the true version of him for the first time. My mind quickly calculates logistics. There's a gun taped against the side of the planter box with radishes, but it's two rows over. Suddenly, I remember: I'd set the butane torch near where I'm standing. Where is it?

"Nothing to say?"

The shovel is small and useless in my hand as I grip it tightly. At a slow pace, I walk around to the front of the plant bed, putting myself in his full view. Right then, I notice the torch between two leafy stalks of vegetation, hidden from Tobias's view. It's at the far edge of where I'm standing. I need to keep his attention on me until Henry returns.

"You're usually much mouthier. Did you come here and grow soft?" asks Tobias, still wearing his all-too-familiar friendly expression, even if the words are sharper, meaner.

"Have you also never wondered why women seem to be in a room with you only when you've trapped them?" I ask idly.

"You always were an ungrateful bitch." There's a dangerous glint in his smile. "Even when my father ensured you were adopted by a nice family, and paid for your education at Oxford. He didn't know I knew you existed, but he always kept an eye on you. Poor Amara," he sneers cruelly. I want to wipe my name out of his mouth. "His precious, forgettable daughter from the woman he loved lifetimes ago. The woman he betrayed *my* mother for."

Valeria Grala. My birth mother. My hands curl over the sides of the cedar bed. She must have been killed by Roman or one of Tatrialny's competitors who knew her connection to him. Questions of how Roman had found me nearly come tumbling out of my mouth, but I let Tobias enjoy his own speech. Let him walk into his own trap.

"He must have thought it was such an amusing coincidence that we both ended up in the same service in London. He was never creative enough to suspect that I'd planned it that way. I worked my ass off to make sure of it."

"How?" I demand.

His eyebrows shoot up. "You never wondered how Emerson came to recruit you? You never even asked?"

Clarity rings like an alarm bell inside me. Isn't that what Emerson had told me that night? *Tobias had recommended you for service... In case you didn't get through, he told me he'd prefer to keep it private... I'd been reminded recently.* If Tobias knew about me despite Roman's attempts to keep it secret, then Tobias had known about me long before I'd met him during my first year of service.

"He told me the night he died."

With satisfaction bordering on sociopathic, Tobias gives me a smug smile.

"I found a way to mention it after a meeting with him," says Tobias. "I wondered if he was making the connection between me and Tatrialny, and I thought I'd nudge him in a better direction. All my life, you've only been a waste of money and a waste of space. He didn't realize I'd see him again that same night, but there's something entertaining about having information other people don't."

"I don't know the feeling," I say. "I wasn't aware of you or Roman. In fact, I went my entire life blissfully unaware of where or who I came from until rather recently. It's almost as if you hardly mattered."

Tobias laughs. "This is excellent. You're only going to make it hurt for yourself later. Henry is going to be disappointed to see the marks I've left on his dead wife. Where is he, by the way?"

"Threatening to kill another member of your family, Tobias?

How unoriginal," I tell him derisively. I don't see Esse, but I worry for her. Feigning a toss of the shove, I casually let my hands lean against the frame of the planter at hip level. I am enough steps away from the torch that if I lunge for it now, Tobias might still reach me before I can light it. Adjusting, I shift my weight on my feet rather than taking a step forward. "What do you get out of this anyway? What do you get out of helping some rich assholes hurt women and children? Surely it's not about money."

"Who gives a shit about the *money*?" he says, as only a rich twat would argue. "There were only two things more powerful than money that I've wanted."

"A larger brain?" I suggest.

He takes a step forward. "Control and attention. My father squandered both by focusing on you and adjusting his business plans because of a latent conscience, despite knowing his competitors were trying to corner the market on him. He had it all, and over and over, he chose wrong."

Market. As if women and children were items on a shelf for men to pluck. White-hot rage bubbles up, but I keep it at a simmer. I'll need it, but not yet.

"A weak answer," I seethe. "You could have control and attention in most illegal industries. What do you gain by using women and children in such a grotesque way? By taking them from their lives?"

"I don't take anyone; I only move people around who have had a bad life to begin with. That's called opportunity. Don't be upset with me for being given different choices," he says in mock innocence with a hand against his collar. "You're quite mad at the wrong person." The gun in his hand points higher, aiming directly at my heart. I hear it in his voice; he will stop at nothing, not when the cost of his ego and his jealousy is on the line. "I'll stop doing it when people stop pursuing it."

I wanted revenge for every child Tatrialny had ever hurt. I wanted to destroy it, and him, if I had to. I would become an incinerator, a wildfire, a burning, raging forest.

Focus. Breathe. I shift my stance again, getting closer. I keep my tone soft, inquisitive. "It's pretty impressive, but how did you know Henry and I were working on the investigation in the first place?"

"You never figured it out?" he asks with an incredulous laugh, distracted by my question. "I was in Warsaw. I was following you, since my plan was to remove you from the equation myself... Then, when I saw you both, I knew it wasn't a coincidence and must have been related to an MI6 investigation. It was my luck the bomb could serve two functions: getting rid of you, and fulfilling Tatrialny's plans."

His words suck all the air out of the warm and humid room. The twins, the other children laughing, all of it has played like a 15-second film on repeat in my mind for over a year, on repeat for the rest of my life. Because of him.

"You fucking *psychopath,*" I spit out. I want to keel over and heave out every drop of guilt and fury and sadness. I shoot my eyes to look him in the face. What a waste of a person, what a waste of life.

"Now that we're beyond pleasantries, you know why I'm here," he says, his loose grin fading. "Stop wasting more time."

"I don't know what you're talking about."

"The *fuck* you don't." A snarl ripples across his features.

"If you're going to kill me anyway, why should I tell you anything?" I point out.

"I can make it quick," he says nicely. He releases the safety and continues to point the gun at me. "Far better than some of the other ideas I had in mind. Tell me where the device is."

"Don't, OK? Please, I don't want to die," I say, affecting acquiescence in the shape of slumping shoulders. "I can take you to where it is, and you can leave. I won't look for you, I promise. You'll have everything you've been wanting: the device and Tatrialny. You'll never see or hear from me again."

"Where the hell is it?" His voice snaps with impatience.

"It's not in here. It's buried in a protective box under a solar panel," I lie, a finger indicating outside. He glances toward the panels, and I move my hand toward the handle of the torch. It grazes against my fingers.

That's when I see Esse. The cat who'd only ever been interested in affection, or snacks, or anyone, really. She's stalking in a way I've never seen before: her claws out, with hair raising straight up on all haunches as if she's preparing to pounce.

And Esse does.

Lunging directly for his face, her snarl is that of a truly wild animal. Tobias fires two shots as he tries to shoot in the direction of the cat. One shot hits a nearby plant bed, and another breaks through the glass. The gun slides across the ground. It lands out of reach, and I can't get to it in time. Without thinking, I grab the butane torch and run at Tobias, whose eyes are getting clawed out.

"ESSE, GO!" I scream, barely stopping long enough before I aim the fire at his legs. For the first fucking time the cat actually obeys, running off. In pain, Tobias is looking for his own claws to find me. His kicks land into my shins, catching me off guard. I cry out and collapse, the torch thrown out of my hands. On its side, the trigger handle is still spitting out fire, an incendiary wound to the garden pots in its path. Tobias pushes himself off the ground faster than I can recover from the sharp pain he'd inflicted. Quickly, I try to grab the torch, but he kicks it out of reach. He kicks me in the stomach. I am not prepared for the sudden loss of air.

His third kick lands in my rib cage so forcefully I think I hear a cracking sound. It hollows out the world. It scoops every thought, every strategy, out of me. He's sitting on my stomach, pinning me to the ground. Lifting his fist above me, he throws one punch after another, the force of his wrath against my cheekbones. Not only his wrath, but his envy of me, his insecurities about being second-best to our father. There is a metallic taste of blood filling my mouth.

There is a wild look in his eyes. I know without a doubt, he is going to kill me.

"You could've made this easier for yourself." He's breathing hard from all the exertion of our struggle. His hands turn into brackets that pin my wrists down. Panic steals my breath and all ability to reason with it. I try to twist and pull free. I kick, my heel accidentally pushing the torch further away. Its head turns toward a stack of plastic plant containers. Then, the new tomato plants, my garden gloves. The torch is ablaze, setting the greenhouse on fire piece by piece.

A terrible fury overcomes me as I watch the place I'd fallen in love with burn. Something else being taken away from me. I become feral. I call on the defensive moves Henry had taught me in my flat in London. Over and over, he'd taught me what to do, and how little strength one needed to exert the kind of force to get someone off me, no matter their size or weight. I know where to make it hurt. Tobias's hands circle my neck. There is only me or him, and he's making me choose.

Without hesitating to consider the pain it will cost me, I thrust my hips up. My knees aim for his back. It catches him off balance in a split second. My right wrist extends, sharply colliding with the heel of my hand against his throat. Coughing in shock, he gasps for breath. He sounds as if he's choking on his own tongue.

Aiming once more with my nails, I dig in to extend the laceration on his face that Esse had started.

Tobias screams in pain.

I twist onto my side and grab the blowtorch. With labored breaths through unbearable pain, I swing my arm back toward him. Flames thrust violently out of the torch. I do it for retribution, for survival. For every child whose future had been stolen away by the greed of men. For the future that had been stolen from me. For the mother who died protecting me, whom I'll never meet.

I will kill for them.

With the torch in my hand, my aim is perfect.

He screams again, his shirt and hands set on fire. Backing away in a frenzy, he tries to roll onto the ground to put it out. It's sheer adrenaline that gets me up off the floor. Latching the door from the inside, I try not to stumble over him. He shrieks as I torch him one final time.

I throw it to the side. He's alive, barely, but he isn't going anywhere. I turn toward the back of the greenhouse. I need to get out.

Branches and stems and roses are aflame around us. All the months of peace I'd made for myself are burning into smoke, clouding up the glass. Wheezing, I suspect he broke a rib that's puncturing my lungs as I search for Esse. There's enough fertilizer inside here that I need to get out before it bursts into flames with me in it. I cough up blood as I collapse in the farthest corner from the door. Arid smoke burns my eyes, my throat, as my fingers search for the pane of glass I'm looking for. I'd repaired it months ago, with a slight modification: a nearly invisible latch on the frame, with four squares of glass swiveling toward the outside. Just big enough for my body to get out in case of emergency. Turning around, I give one last scream for the cat.

"ESSE!" I scream her name with all the air left in my lungs. "ESSE!"

She finally hops over the last raised bed and onto the ground. The bed topples, everything weak and dying. Esse runs out of the greenhouse through the safety door. As I crawl on my hands and knees, Henry is pulling me out. He picks me up and carries me away from the glasshouse into the field.

"Amara—oh, God—"

"I need—" I'm struggling to breathe, as if I am drowning underwater. "I can't—"

Understanding the source of my struggle, he sets me down against a tree so I'm at an incline. It only marginally lessens the feeling of my chest being punched in, but it doesn't make it worse.

"I've already called the *pompiers*, both trucks will be here soon. Just hold on for me." His words rush out all at once. I blink up at the fear etching itself between his brows as he holds me close.

"I'm so sorry I left you here alone—" he says. Just then, the greenhouse explodes. Henry clutches me inward to shield against the glass shattering nearby. In the distance, I can hear sirens. We watch everything burn as we wait for their arrival. Tobias had stopped screaming. With a groan, the metal no longer able to withstand the heat, the greenhouse collapses, everything inside it now in death's possession. The fire and smoke reach their bitter peak toward the sky, wrapping my grief inside its infernal hands.

CHAPTER THIRTY-SEVEN

MARSEILLES, FRANCE, FOUR DAYS LATER

A few days pass as I lie in the recovery ward of a hospital in Marseilles. Henry told me I'd slept for two days straight, and I can see in his eyes how little he'd slept while I'd been unconscious. He never leaves me. Just sits in a chair next to my bed, his hand in mine. I've been too tired to talk or dissect what happened. Each day, sleep engulfs me. I must have nightmares, because in between states of consciousness, I find him watching me until I fall asleep again.

By the fourth morning, I'm sick of sleeping, and I try to pull myself out of the heavy depths of medication. Henry is half bent over the hospital bed, sleeping in the chair. His lashes rest on his cheeks. The blinds behind him are open, with a clear view of the boat docks. I try to shift without disturbing him, but he wakes anyway. He straightens with worry, then relief floods his face when he realizes I'm sitting up.

"Let me help."

Without waiting, he adjusts another pillow behind me. He returns to sit in his chair and holds my hand.

"I wish I'd killed him myself."

"You can't be first at everything." My mouth twists, but so does my heart at the reminder of what I'd done.

He rests his forehead on our hands. "I only regret I wasn't there sooner."

"He suffered," I whisper. "I ended it, and I'm glad he's dead."

"Mind if I come in?"

Just past Henry toward the door is James. The moment I see her, I begin to cry. James stands with two other officers, their backs to the door. Henry lets go of my hand and stands.

"You're here," I say.

James takes long strides into the room, her short red hair brushing over her shoulder. She sits where Henry has been, and her green eyes shine as they look into mine.

"I'm so glad you're okay," whispers James. Her green eyes are glassy. "Henry called me, and I wanted to be here right away. There was something I needed to take care of first."

"He's been here taking care of me," I tell her reassuringly. "Mostly I've been sleeping, though, so you haven't missed much."

"Do you think you'd be up to talking about what happened?"

"The doctor says she has a broken rib, a fractured wrist, and multiple contusions," Henry interjects. "She needs her rest."

I give him the side eye.

"He's only worried about you," says James with reluctant admiration. "But it's ultimately your call."

"I want to."

"You sure?" James watches me.

I nod. "I'm sure."

"Then I'll bring her in," James nods to one of the agents standing in the hall.

"Who?" Asks Henry, frowning.

A woman in a two-piece suit sweeps into the room. Her hair is a high, light blonde bun. When her eyes meet mine, I can immediately see the sharp intelligence behind them. Henry has been standing next to James, and his arms go rigid at his side. The woman scans the room, her eyes resting on me.

"You're Sophie Vester," I say, staring back.

"I am," she says, her mouth curling up. Indicating to the chair James is sitting in, she says, "May I?" though it isn't really a question.

"I called Sophie after Henry called me the day you were taken to the hospital," explains James. Her red hair sways as she swivels her head to look at me. "He briefed me on everything about Tobias, Tatrialny, and the device. I contacted the director general of security service at MI5, who escalated things to the home secretary."

"Emerson suspected an agent in MI6 was leaking information to Tatrialny, and it was his idea to infiltrate." Sophie sits, her legs crossing as she studies me. I feel a familiar pang in my chest at his name. "On the chance there might be an assassination attempt, he pulled me from a different foreign assignment and put me to surveil the syndicate. Only three people knew about the covert operation. It was right after the terrorist attack in Warsaw, and I was instructed to get close to Tobias. As a precaution, Emerson considered the possibility that the double agent could be Henry, given his field experience, but he was more convinced it was someone else. That's when Tobias mentioned you," she says, a hand waving in my direction. "Emerson wanted to know if there was a connection between the two of you. He was sure of it, but couldn't quite put his finger on why."

"Then why was your name given to me by my informant?" demanded Henry. "He died getting me that information, saying you were rising the ranks quickly in Tatrialny to pass the bills within Parliament—"

"You are correct. Emerson knew he needed to establish credibility with whoever was committing treason, which is why he brought me in. I had to remain in a less visible role in order to find out who had infiltrated. Tobias caught on because he disseminated conflicting information." She looks between us grimly. "Antoni gave bad information and was killed by Tatrialny for it. I'm sorry. I liked him. He died honorably."

"How did Emerson know it wasn't us?" I ask.

"Because he told me himself he suspected Tobias, for many reasons, but specifically because of some information about his background he hadn't been forthcoming about when he'd been hired as an agent. He'd never disclosed that he spoke Polish, which Emerson found odd, given that, after some more digging, it turned out Tobias had been born there. Against my advice, Emerson kept this information close to protect the investigation," she says.

Henry looks to me behind Sophie and James, an invisible question hanging between us.

Do I trust her?

Sophie's eyes have a subtle trace of sorrow underneath her stoic exterior. I believe her. Everything she's saying aligns with what I know and what Tobias revealed in that greenhouse. I give Henry a small nod, then return my attention to Sophie. James takes out recording tech and sets it on the bed.

For the next hour, I tell them everything. All that Tobias had told me, and all Henry and I had learned over the past several months. The bomb, the meetings with Emerson, the greenhouse on fire. I ignore the squeeze of pain at my side to tell it.

Henry leans against one of the windows, listening with arms crossed. After I finish, my eyes start to become heavy.

"I think we're done," says Henry firmly.

"I agree," adds James, and pockets the recorder.

Sophie peers at me. "When you're in better shape to travel, let's get you settled back into the office and—"

"I don't want to go back to London," I say.

"Oh?" Sophie asks in surprise.

"Will I be prosecuted in any way?" I ask hesitantly.

"No, of course not," says Sophie with a shake of her head. "You won't even be asked to testify in this case publicly. This is classified information. Including the full roster of names in foreign governments and media that we've obtained."

"You got it?" Henry asks, uncrossing his arms.

"The whole damn thing," says Sophie with flashing satisfaction. "Thanks to James and the director of MI5."

"That list is longer than the required reading at my son's school," says James, giving a grin.

"I want to stay in France, then," I say with relief. "If possible."

Sophie looks between me and Henry. "You both will be afforded all the protection MI6 can provide."

"I also want to stay in the cottage," I add.

Sophie sighs. "Any other demands?"

"That's it for now, I think." I smile.

"We'll get to work starting tonight to remove you from the system," says Sophie as she stands. Turning to Henry, she reaches to shake his hand.

"I imagine you'll also be included in this protection?"

"I go where she goes," says Henry.

"A loss to the agency," says Sophie most sincerely. They shake hands, and she gives me one final glance before leaving the room. James stands up to leave as well. Her eyes fill with tears as she leans down to gently place her arms around mine in goodbye.

"I searched for you everywhere," says James, her voice cracking. "I am so glad you have someone like him looking after you."

"We'll find a way to stay in contact as much as we can," I tell her. My eyes sting, and my voice comes out as a croak from exhaustion and tears. "I'll add it to my list of demands of Chief Vester," I say, smiling through tears that cling to my lashes like drops of rain.

James nods, wiping at the corners of both eyes. She makes sure Henry has Sophie's secure line, then quietly closes the door behind her.

Henry returns to the chair. Without much choice, my body is relenting to the heavy persuasion of exhaustion. He leans in to kiss me gently on the cheek.

"We get to stay here," he says, leaning in to kiss me gently on the cheek. "We'll rebuild the greenhouse. We get more time now, together. As it should be."

His words balloon my relief, my joy, to be with him. "I love you," I whisper.

"I love you this day as much as the first day," he whispers back.

"It's not a competition."

His laugh is a deep rumble I can feel all the way down to our interlacing hands. Outside the window of the hospital, the sun is a bright orb in the sky, the day alight with more than what I'd allowed myself to dream of in a long while: the future.

Acknowledgements

The inception of this book came from inspiration of two stories that were on a 24/7 scroll in my brain for years: *Under The Tuscan Sun* and *Mr. & Mrs. Smith.* While both films are seemingly different genres, my imagination threaded between them two questions: What can starting over in a new place look like? And what if the path there began because of someone you believed you hated for good reason?

There's nothing I apparently love more than painting myself into a corner and seeing what happens next. So while I knew I wanted the book set against the backdrop of a romantic landscape in a European country, I wanted the intrigue of an espionage thriller plot. Although the complexity of this story did not deter me, having resources to better capture the countries depicted in this book were a crucial aspect of aiming to tell a good story. I'm immensely grateful for those who took time out of their lives to help me understand the places they call or have called home.

Thank you Sam and Paul Fournier, for your support and expertise to ensure I captured the beauty, and culture of the South of

France.

Thank you Jeannine Hightower for bolstering my admiration for Polish culture and history, your lived experience of living in Warsaw was the final puzzle piece.

Thank you Jonathon Grant, for the lovely perspective and entertaining details of London, as well as your wonderful voice notes that captured your experience and humor in a way emails could never.

Lauren, I am so honored to have your artistic talent grace my book covers, thank you for perfectly bringing my vision to life.

Thank you Miranda, for your copywriting eye and expertise, you are an excellent leader of my punctuation support group of one.

Thank you to my fabulous author coven, I mean author's group—Sydney and Elizabeth. Our monthly meet-ups are the best emotional support a writer could ever have.

To the friends who listen, cheer me on, and are first in line to order a copy of my books: Steph, Dar, Kristin, Jenny, Virva, Eva Claire, and Casie. Thank you for being part of what makes being an author feel real.

And finally, to J. Put this in a frame on a wall: you were right. Nothing is ever wasted.

RESOURCES

Human trafficking is a serious and active risk, especially for vulnerable youth in the welfare system. I have included resources that offer information, statistical insight, and ways to protect at-risk children and youth.

https://www.justice.gov/humantrafficking/resources

https://polarisproject.org/myths-facts-and-statistics

https://www.uscis.gov/humanitarian/victims-of-human-trafficking-and-other-crimes/resources-for-victims-of-human-trafficking-and-other-crimes

Book Club Guide

This reading group guide for *One Night in Warsaw* includes discussion questions and ideas to enhance your book club. The questions are intended to delve into topics and varied perspectives from the story.

1. The opening scene involving the iron gate of the cottage is mirrored in chapter two in front of the orphanage. What were your impressions about the similarities between those two moments?

2. It's revealed Amara does not know her birth parents, and her adoptive parents have passed away. What do you think this says about her outlook in life, and her ability to be close to others? Do you think her approach hinders or hurts her?

3. After Henry reveals Emerson's possible involvement with Tatrialny, Amara struggles to reconcile facts against her view of him as a sort of father figure. Do you think this contributes to her resentment of Henry? Do you think Henry is aware of that possibility, and if so, what does this

say about his feelings toward Amara?

4. *One Night in Warsaw* plays with the concept of geography as it relates to emotional concepts. What do you think being in the cottage in the South of France says about Amara's emotional state? What does London say about her emotional state?

5. Amara finds it difficult getting close to others, but her friendship with James is conveyed as important from the beginning. What are your thoughts of the decision to withhold depicting that closeness until the last chapter? What are the ways doing so captures the concept of isolation throughout the story?

6. The central theme of who Amara is rests within the story she tells herself about abandonment and grief. What is one word you'd use to describe who she becomes by the end of the story?

7. After the bomb in Warsaw, Amara's resolve to stop Tatrialny is elevated by the loss of two young sisters. What does the decisions she makes after that day say about her, and her past?

8. After Amara sees Henry with another woman, it throws them in a turmoil of miscommunication and distrust and

off the trajectory of happiness. As the story explores her identity and her past, what reflections do you have about the intersection of forgiveness and the fear of vulnerability?

9. What was your favorite scene or moment from part two? How does it tie in with the love story between Amara and Henry?

10. By part three it's revealed just how much Amara has sacrificed in order to protect the device. What is a defining moment in the story where you feel she accepts her role in keeping it safe? What about that moment moves toward or away from the broader subject of putting others above oneself for the greater good?

11. Amara assumes Henry to be, "smug and arrogant" (page 26). What are one of the moments in the story that you think begins to convince her otherwise?

12. The portrayal of Tobias envy and Amara's grief manifest in different ways; how would you describe the way those emotions overlap? The way they differ?

Starling Darling Bonus

In this striking and suspenseful story of love, mothers, and memory, *Starling Darling* is Lucia's journey to reclaim what's hers and let go of what's not. Can she find a way toward an unwritten future by forgiving her mother without abandoning herself?

Lucia Starling gets a phone call that changes her life: Her mother has died, and in the wake of it is an inheritance of an 18th century necklace, and memories of a mother she hasn't spoken with in five years.

Neither of which she knows what to do with, except, perhaps to escape New York and leave the country. Far from home at least, she won't have to face her father's sorrow, or her own guilt.

When her mother's necklace is robbed from her hotel room in Rome, Lucia suspects the culprit to be a mysterious foreigner. When she discovers his identity, she's faced with an impossible voyage. Lucia must decide to confront her past or her future; return to New York City, or find the necklace before it's sold on the black market and lost forever?

One thing is for certain: her mother's necklace is only the beginning.

Download your FREE sneak peek.

About the Author

Erica Vipond is the author of slow burn romantic thrillers, including *Starling Darling*, and the espionage thriller, *One Night in Warsaw*. She has a B.A. in English, and a love for studying languages. She is currently hard at work on her debut romantasy that is a Count of Monte Cristo reimagining about sisterhood, betrayal and revenge.

When not writing, you can find her ice skating, binging kdramas, and spending time in her garden.

Join for publishing news, & giveaways:

www.ingramcontent.com/pod-product-compliance
Lightning Source LLC
Chambersburg PA
CBHW071757040826
49266CB00047B/457
9798218828998